DAUGHTERS
of
COPPER WOMAN

Be safe

Ask questions

Listen well

Anticipate and adapt

Gather stories

Find magic

Erik

DAUGHTERS
of
COPPER WOMAN

Anne Cameron

HARBOUR PUBLISHING

Harbour Publishing Co. Ltd.
P.O. Box 219, Madeira Park, BC, V0N 2H0
www.harbourpublishing.com

Front cover painting by Chester (Chaz) F. Patrick
Cover and interior design by Roger Handling, Terra Firma
Printed and bound in Canada

About the cover illustration: The image of the elderly woman is a reflection, a spirit, of the younger woman, as she looks back on her youth. The younger woman looks back in time, thinking of her sisters. Each of them, before reaching her destination, gave her food and wisdom to Copper Woman so that she would carry on. The copper moon overlooking the bay is a reminder of arrival and new life.

Chester Patrick, a Gitxsan artist, was born in 1958 and grew up in Gitanmaax, BC. At an early age he was schooled as a principal dancer with 'Ksan Performing Arts and later attended the Gitanmaax School of Northwest Coast Indian Art. Patrick is an accomplished carver, working principally in yellow cedar to create masks, spoons, poles and flat relief pieces, and he is also a painter. Much of his work is inspired by Gitxan stories, legends, songs and dances. His carvings, paintings and illustrations can be found in galleries, private collections and public institutions throughout North America and Europe.

Harbour Publishing acknowledges financial support from the Government of Canada through the Book Publishing Industry Development Program and the Canada Council for the Arts, and from the Province of British Columbia through the BC Arts Council and the Book Publishing Tax Credit.

THE CANADA COUNCIL | LE CONSEIL DES ARTS
FOR THE ARTS | DU CANADA
SINCE 1957 | DEPUIS 1957

BRITISH
COLUMBIA
ARTS COUNCIL
We acknowledge the support of the Province of British Columbia through the British Columbia Arts Council

Library and Archives Canada Cataloguing in Publication

Cameron, Anne, 1938–
    Daughters of Copper Woman

    ISBN 1-55017-245-X

    1. Nootka women—Fiction. 2. Nootka Indians—Folklore. 3. Indians of North America—British Columbia—Vancouver Island—Folklore. 2. Indians of North America—British Columbia—Vancouver Island—History. I. Title
PS8565.U24D38 2002   C813'.54   C2001-911669-1
PR9199.3.H75D3 2002

With gratitude to the Nuu-chah-nulth people and my adopted family in Ahousat, especially Audrey Atleo, who shares with me the name given us by her Big Nan. We are Shaula.

In memory of Mary Little, Margaret Atleo, "Blind" Mother Thomas, Pearl Pointe, Annie Yorke, James Adams, David Frank, John Jacobson and NaiNai Russ, Elsie Irvine, Lily Busk and my mother, Annie Cameron.

For my children:
Marianne, Alex, Erin and Pierre, with love, and with thanks for all you have taught me, shown me and demonstrated to me.

For my grandchildren:
Sarah, David, Daniel, Terry, Sheldon, Jenelle, Andy, Charlie, Chrissie, Joan and whoever it is we're waiting to meet...

And especially for Eleanor. Whatever your little heart desires, kiddo. Two decades and, for what it's worth to you, I'd do it all again in a heartbeat. I love you.

CONTENTS

PREFACE

The stories that inspired this book were taught to me by the generous and wonderful elder women of the Nuu-chah-nulth Nation, who are my friends and who for years were my neighbours on Vancouver Island. They have a tradition of sharing and I am fascinated by tales, myths, legends, poetry and song, so they told me the stories. And they instructed me to put the stories on paper and have them published, for all of our children and grandchildren, but especially for the ones who have been deprived of some of the healing aspects of their grandmothers' culture.

From these women I learned creation stories about First Mother, who was made of the earth on which we stand, in whose veins ran blood as salty as the sea, whose hair is as the grass, whose pubic hair is as the moss, whose bones and teeth are as the shells and whose children became scattered, and spread out to cover the earth. And I learned that we are all cousins, because we are all grandchildren of First Mother. This earth is our home, and we have very little time in which to learn how to treat her with respect.

The stories have great resonance for me, a mother and grandmother of Celtic heritage, and the stories went on to touch a nerve in women throughout the world. Since 1981, when *Daughters of Copper Woman* was first published by a small collective of women, this quiet little revolutionary work has been translated into many languages, reprinted many times, and brought me mail from all over the world. I am gratified that so many readers are making the connections between all of the creation myths, and finding the inner peace that comes with beginning to find and integrate the fragments.

SONG FOR THE DEAD

The numbers with which the *Song for the Dead* is introduced come from the memorizers of the warrior society; from their perspective, a man had multiple wives, whereas the women memorizers' view was that several women shared one husband.

The warrior society drew its members from the nobility and the royalty. Commoners and slaves represented two other levels of society, and their numbers, like the numbers of the women and children, were lost in epidemics. Those who would have memorized their history, their family lineage, their population, did not survive the many uncontrollable diseases.

In the eighty-five years between Captain Cook's visit in 1788 and the Royal Fellowship census in 1863, the Nuu-chah-nulth nations were decimated.

The Nitinat once numbered more than 8,000 warriors; fewer than 35 remained.

Yuquot, once home to 2,000 men, their wives, children and slaves, plus commoners and their wives and children, had less than 200 people.

In Clayoquot Sound more than 1,000 warriors, their wives, children and slaves, plus the general population of commoners, had been reduced to 135.

Tahsis, with more than 2,000 fighting men, their wives, children and slaves, plus the general population, was reduced to 60 people.

Civilization brought measles, whooping cough, chicken pox, diphtheria, smallpox, tuberculosis, syphilis, gonorrhea, alcohol and influenza.

We are beating the drums
and singing songs
having a great feast for the dead
for our children are gone
and none remain.
> Come back my nephew we miss you
> Come back my daughter we miss you
> Come back my son we miss you
> Come back our lost ones we miss you

Come back we are lonely
Where have you gone
Come back we are lonely
Where have you gone
> Come back we are weeping
> Where have you gone
> Come back we are asking
> Where have you gone

Come back my brother
Come back my sister
Come back my father
Come back my mother
> We will sing a song for you
> We will follow the river to the sea
> And add our tears to the waves

The tide will rise
The tide will fall
The night will come
The night will go
> You will not come
> You who are gone.

Where did you go?

> We are singing our sorrow
> We are singing our grief
> We are singing our farewell
>   and our puzzlement

Why did you go?

COPPER WOMAN

The Creator took handfuls of dirt and on the skeleton fashioned a body, which was then encased in skin, made from the skin of the Creator and the same colour as copper...

The Creator made four levels of reality: earth, under-the-earth, ocean and under-the-sea. And then the Creator, who is neither male nor female, man nor woman, but both, and something more than either, more than both, populated each reality.

First the Creator took sticks and twigs and from them fashioned a child. Be careful, now, the Creator warned Stick Child. Do not play too close to the fire and be sure to keep yourself damp and supple. Stick Child agreed, and for a time all was well. Stick Child dipped herself in the calm, shallow fresh water every morning and made her prayers to the Creator. She played in the warm, shallow salt water and ran happily in the rain when it fell from the sky.

But Stick Child was forgetful and careless, and she began to neglect her purification baths, began to spend hour after hour in the hot sun without soaking herself, and so she became dry and brittle, no longer supple, no longer able to move gracefully and easily, and one day she stumbled, lurched sideways and staggered into the fire, where she was consumed.

The Creator tried again. The Creator took grass and moss, leaves and vines and fashioned Grass Child. Do not play too close to the fire and be sure to keep yourself damp and supple, the Creator said. And when the storms begin to blow, take yourself into your house and stay there. Grass Child agreed, and for a time, all was well. Grass Child kept herself damp and supple, she was very careful around the fire and never went too close to the flames, and in almost every way she obeyed the instructions of the Creator. She was in the hills, gathering ripe berries when the sky began to fill with dark clouds. Grass Child knew a storm was coming, she knew she should hurry home, but the berries were ripe and sweet, and Grass Child knew that after the rain the berries would be soggy, almost tasteless, so she lingered, gathering the precious berries in her woven basket. She was only partway home when the storm hit. Rain fell in torrents and the wind shrieked and howled. Grass Child was buffeted and battered. The vines holding her together snapped and she was blown in every direction at once.

The Creator took mud and with it made Mud Child. Be careful, the Creator told Mud Child. Do not go too close to the fire, keep yourself damp and supple, but do not go into the fresh water nor into the salt water. Mud Child promised, but she was not particularly bright. She was not as careful as she should have been; she stood too long with one foot in a puddle. Her foot dissolved and left her limping on her ankle. Another time she peeked out of her house during a storm and held her hand under the stream of water running from the edge of the roof. Her hand dissolved and fell off at the wrist. Mud Child tried to scoop up her hand by stepping out of her house and reaching down to gather up the mud that had been her own hand, so that she could put it back on her arm. The rain fell on her and washed away her head. She crumpled and became part of a mud puddle.

The Creator took the shells of the sea and the minerals of the rocks and from them fashioned a skeleton. Then the Creator took the salt water of the ocean and made from it blood, to run in veins. The Creator took handfuls of dirt and on the skeleton fashioned a body, which was then encased in skin, made from the skin of the Creator and the same colour as copper. Under her arms and between her legs the Creator placed soft-scented moss. A brain was added, and a heart; organs were placed inside and then eyes to see. The form was given the senses of touch, taste, smell, sight and hearing, and then the Creator trapped the wind and placed it in her lungs and she became First Woman, she became Copper Woman.

Alone she found shelter and alone she found food. She picked oysters, dug clams and ate them raw, she found birds' eggs, cracked them open and ate the rich contents. She picked berries, she dug roots, and she survived.

When the summer storms raged, Copper Woman sat inside her shelter and watched as the thunder rumbled and the lightning flashed. A tall cedar tree was struck; it snapped and fell, burning, near the mouth of the shelter. Copper Woman dared to rush out, grab pieces of wood, race into her shelter with them and then get a branch, still burning, and add it. With the power of the lightning trapped and tamed, her shelter became warmer and brighter, and her life improved. She could cook food now, and enjoy it more.

She learned to weave weirs to lay out at high tide, and when the water went down at low tide, caught in the weirs were fish to be speared or netted, or sometimes grabbed with bare hands, then taken back to the shelter and cooked.

She Endured. Endured and survived. Marginally, perhaps, but it is not required of us that we live well. Throughout the storms of autumn, throughout the long, wet winter, and even when the snow lay deep on the mountain and ice blocked the streams, she Endured. Only an idiot could have starved on the coast and Copper Woman was no idiot. She learned which seaweeds were good, she learned how to swim, how to dive down and gather abalone, sea urchin and crab, she learned how to find, catch and cook ducks and other birds. Every month she had her moon cycle, and every month she wondered why, for there was nobody else and she had no idea at all about companionship or procreation.

Alone she built a small wooden house. Alone she learned to harvest Tutsup the sea urchin, Ya-is the butter clam, Hetchen the littleneck clam, Ah-sam the crab, Um-echt the horse clam and So-ha the spring salmon. She learned to eat the meat and make clothes from Kich-tlatz the fur seal. Alone she learned Tut-lukh the sea lion was not to be approached unwarily.

In the time of the first autumn storms, the Creator sent a craft of supernaturals to teach Copper Woman how to survive on a better level than she had been able to find for herself. Coming from the setting sun, riding down the golden slide that cuts across the water just before the blanket of nightfall, the supernaturals came to teach her what all humankind must know to live more fully. The supernaturals taught her about the rhythm of the drum beating in her chest, taught her to dance to the pulse in her veins, taught her to sing and to laugh.

She who had been alone for so long was no longer alone, but shared her meals with supernaturals who had become her friends. She who had been alone and known nothing else now had company and more than company. She had companionship and more.

But this was not the time or place for the supernaturals to stay, and as they got in their craft and prepared to return to their own home, Copper Woman began to weep. Bitterly she cried, for loneliness is a bitter thing and an acrid taste in our mouths, more bitter when you think you have been freed from it and find it returning again. So much did she cry, her very head began to drain of all fluid, and as tears fell from her eyes, from her nose fell great amounts of thick mucus. Tears and mucus and from her mouth saliva, and her face swelled as the waters of loneliness poured. From her nose an enormous cluster of mucus strands fell onto the sand and lay at her feet, and so great was the cluster that even in her pathetic state, Copper Woman was aware of it and grew ashamed, and shy. Trying to conquer her wailing, she kicked sand over the mess to bury it, hide it, return it to the earth.

The supernatural women told her not to feel shame, not to bury the snot but to save it, even cherish it, and when she had learned to accept even this most gross evidence of her own mortality, then from the acceptance would come the means whereby she would never again be alone, never again be lonely.

They told her that those times when body secretions flow, those times when a woman answers the call of the moon, are holy and sacred times, times for prayer and contemplation.

Copper Woman did as she was told. Not understanding, but having faith, she scooped up the mess in a mussel shell and put it with her magic things. A few days later she noticed that the sand in the shell was moving. She looked closely and saw a small, incomplete thing twisting uncomfortably in the shell. Copper Woman carefully placed what was in the mussel shell in a larger shell, a shell of Um-echt the horse clam. Every day she watched and became aware that the small living incomplete thing was growing something that looked like a miniature of the neck of the horse clam. Soon the small figure was too large to be comfortable in the shell of Um-echt, so she put it in a shell of Tutsup the sea urchin. But in only a day or two she moved it again, for beneath the thing that looked like the neck of Um-echt, this creature was developing small versions of Tutsup, and Copper Woman did not want the spines of the sea urchin to grow between the legs of her little friend, for then how would he walk? So she put him in the shell of Ah-sam the crab. For a few weeks he was happy, although, like Ah-sam, he would grab at her with his hands and not want to let go. Copper Woman put her little manikin in a bed made of fur from Tut-lukh the sea lion and he was happy enough, even though on his face he grew whiskers like Tut-lukh and on parts of his chest and belly the soft fur of the big animal. And his voice became deep and he roared with jealousy when Copper Woman spent too much time admiring something else.

One night the snot boy left his bed of fur from Tut-lukh and crawled in bed with Copper Woman. He fastened his mouth, like the mouth of Ah-sam, on her mouth, and his hands, grasping like the claws of Ah-sam, felt for her breasts. Copper Woman knew she could easily destroy this impertinent snot boy, but she also felt responsible for him and sorry for him for being such an incomplete collection of traits from a number of sea creatures. Had not the sea saved her, provided her with nourishment? Had not the supernaturals come from the sea and told her that this strange thing would be the means whereby she would never again be alone? Besides, his mouth on hers was pleasant, and his hands, though demanding, were not hurtful and caused a warmth in her belly. A warmth that grew until the part of him made from the neck of Um-echt and the parts of him that resembled Tutsup began to come alive and grow, and she welcomed Um-echt into her body and held the snot boy close to her, closer, until the lonely feeling almost—but not quite—went away, and she felt her body swelling, filling as if with the moon itself.

The snot boy cried out, not the deep voice of Tut-lukh but a cry much like that of Qui-na the gull, and then the manikin held onto her and shook as if the autumn gales were within him. Copper Woman soothed him and held him close and wondered if the loneliness would ever totally go. Many times thereafter she held the snot boy close and fixed her mouth on his, used the magic of her hands to waken the two small Tutsup, and once they were awake the Um-echt part entered her, seeking, exploring, taking her almost—almost—from loneliness.

MOWITA

And Copper Woman looked at her daughter and felt the loneliness diminish until it was no larger than a small round pebble on the beach...

Copper Woman was living with Snot Boy, the incomplete manikin, in the place where the supernaturals had come to give her knowledge. She taught the small, strange creature as much as she could, but he never seemed to learn properly. When he built a weir, there was always one part of it not properly made, and many of the fish would escape. When he built a fire it was either too hot or not hot enough, and often he would burn himself. When he was through using a thing, he would leave it, never remembering to put it away where he could find it again, and sometimes he would forget to come home when the meal was ready, then would complain bitterly if his food was overdone or cold. Copper Woman would tease him, make him forget his ill humour, laugh with him and often she would sing for him, for she was less lonely with him than she had been when she was alone.

Her breasts grew large and tender, her belly filled until it looked as if the moon itself was trapped inside, and one day, movement within her told her she was no longer one person, but two, that there was another living inside her body. Copper Woman prayed daily that this other would not be incomplete like Snot Boy, but an entire person, capable of responsibility and attention to detail. Often she felt frightened and wondered about her own ability to care for this new person, and once or twice she chafed to think she was no longer free to be herself, but had to think in terms of another.

One night, with much pain and blood, there came from her a small version of herself, but altered. The copper skin was darker and the hair black, even blacker than that of Ku-ka-was the hair seal. The eyes were more slanted, almost like those of the cormorant, which had no other name yet and would get its name much later when the blindness was taken from it. And Copper Woman looked at her daughter and felt the loneliness diminish until it was no larger than a small round pebble on the beach. Her breasts ached with a pulsation like that of the waves on the beach, and when she had cleaned the blood from her daughter and the mucus from the small nose and mouth, she wept with thanks for the secret magic the supernaturals had given her. Knowing the secret, she had been able to lick clean her child and not feel revulsion. Rather, she felt that again, but in a different way, she was giving life to herSelf. When she held her child close, to warm her and make her welcome, the small head turned and the soft mouth closed around Copper Woman's swollen and darkened nipple. The small pebble of loneliness vanished and a feeling even stronger than those awakened by Snot Boy filled Copper Woman until it was as if the supernaturals themselves had entered into her, through her to her milk, and from the milk to the child, so she named the child Mowita, knowing she would one day be a matriarch.

Snot Boy did not pay much attention to Mowita. Sometimes he played with her, sometimes he even held her and spoke softly to her, but mostly he went about his own affairs. Incomplete, he could catch fish, but it was Copper Woman, and later Mowita, who knew how to cook, smoke and cure. Time and again they showed Snot Boy how to do it, but he would laugh and say he had no time for such bothersome details, and he would leave, laughing. He could catch Mowitch the deer, but was useless curing the hide or cooking the meat.

When Mowita was walking and laughing and beginning to make words, Copper Woman gave life to a son, like Snot Boy, but not quite so incomplete. And when this child was walking, there was another, again a girl. To her daughters Copper Woman taught the secrets, to her sons she tried to teach more than Snot Boy would ever know. Many children had Copper Woman, and their laughter rang clearly, riding on the wind, climbing to the heavens as does the smoke of a fire, and life for them was pleasant.

QOLUS THE CHANGEABLE

One day Qolus told Thunderbird she wanted to live on earth, for it seemed there was more to do than sit or fly. Thunderbird said the decision was hers to make, but she must remember that when one changes form, one changes totally...

There are four kingdoms to reality. The kingdom of earth, that of the underground, that under the sea and that of the heavens.

The kingdom of the heavens was ruled by Thunderbird. When he opened his eyes the sun shone, when he ruffled his feathers the wind blew, when he waved his great wings the colours flashed and we called it lightning, and when he slapped his wings together came the noise we call thunder.

Thunderbird ruled with his wife Qolus. Like Thunderbird she was made of bright feathers, although she had no horns on her head, and she, who was the equal of Thunderbird, had little to do but fly around the heavens with Thunderbird, keeping the clouds in their places, sending rain when it was needed, and waiting. Waiting. Waiting.

Qolus spent much time watching Copper Woman and her children. Especially Mowita, the oldest, the first born, the most special of gifts. Mowita was growing now to womanhood but was still a girl, and her graceful movements and happy laughter warmed Qolus and made her happy.

One day Qolus told Thunderbird she wanted to live on earth, for it seemed there was more to do than sit or fly. Thunderbird said the decision was hers to make, but she must remember that when one changes form, one changes totally.

Qolus still wanted to leave the kingdom of the heavens and go to earth. So she changed form. So completely did she change form that she arrived on earth as Mah Teg Yelah, the first man. Snot Boy, the incomplete, would never be a man and the sons of Copper Woman were still little boys, and not as many lived as had been born, for some had died from fighting or recklessness.

Mah Teg Yelah looked on the daughters of earth and considered them fair. He set to building a house larger than any on earth, for he wished to impress the daughters of Copper Woman. But when the house was half built, he found the ridgepole too heavy to lift into place, so he called on Thunderbird to help. Coming to earth, his magic feathers flashing, Thunderbird first changed himself into human form so that he could talk, and when he understood the problem, he changed back to himself and took the ridgepole in his mighty talons and lifted it in place. Copper Woman and her daughters watched all of this and knew Mah Teg Yelah was magical, and Copper Woman was pleased.

When the house was built and Mah Teg Yelah asked Mowita to be his wife, Copper Woman did not disagree. Mowita herself was not interested in spending her life caring for an incomplete one like Snot Boy or her brothers, and so she agreed and became the wife of Mah Teg Yelah, who had been Qolus the Changeable, wife of Thunderbird. They had four sons, all magical like their mother and father, and the sons grew well and quickly.

Time to those in the heavens is not as Time to those on earth and Mah Teg Yelah pined for the skies, for it seemed to take forever to do anything on earth. Still, he had his wife and children to care for so he stayed.

Thunderbird himself was lonely, though Time for him passed more quickly, and so it was that the sons were nearly men before the loneliness began to affect Thunderbird, for he missed Qolus and knew she was not totally happy as Mah Teg Yelah.

Thunderbird began to weep. He did not intend to cause any harm to anyone, but he was lonely and his Qolus was not happy, and so Thunderbird wept. Copper Woman told Mowita the rain would not stop until each finger on either hand had seen four—magic four—days of rain.

Mowita set to work with Mah Teg Yelah and covered the entire log house with pitch. Her brothers laughed at her. Her sisters helped her. And as the water rose and the house began to float, the sisters of Mowita entered the waterproof house, too. Copper Woman said she did not have to go into the house, which was getting very crowded; she would be safe with her magic. It was Time, she said, for her skin to split anyway, Time for her to allow her children to go off on their own so that they would not stay tied to her forever. So she left her bag of meat and bones on the beach and went to visit with her friends the supernaturals.

For days the house floated, then Mah Teg Yelah sent Raven out to see if the land was still there. Raven returned wet and tired and said there was no place even to rest, that everything was water. Some days later Mah Teg Yelah sent the Raven out again and this time she brought back the promise of life, a sprig of cedar. Still the water covered all but the tops of the tallest trees and there was no place for Raven to rest. A few days later Raven was again sent out, and this time she came back, flew to a window and dropped in a sprig of hemlock, then flew away again. When Raven flew away, all inside the house knew it was safe outside and so they opened the pitch-sealed door. Indeed, there were again mountains, valleys, rivers, lakes and grassy ground beneath their feet. And from that time on, hemlock has been used as protection against drowning.

The animals in the pitch-sealed house ran outside happily, then the daughters of Copper Woman prepared to leave. But the sons of Mowita and Mah Teg Yelah said they wished to go with the women, and so they did, four couples going off in four different directions, and from them came all the people of the world. From the survivors of the flood came the parents of the black people, the parents of the yellow people, the parents of the white people and the parents of the brown-skinned people, and so we are all related, for we all come from the belly of Copper Woman.

Mowita looked at Mah Teg Yelah as their sons left with her sisters to populate the earth, and she knew he yearned for the heavens. She told him it was Time, his duties as a father were finished, his duties as husband were fulfilled, and he was happy. Calling on Thunderbird he changed back into Qolus, and Mowita watched Qolus fly upward to join her husband.

Then Mowita sat and wondered if now she, too, would be alone. She wept to not have her sons, her sisters, her husband, her mother. And after she had wept, she rose and set about the task of establishing a new life for herself, and for many days and weeks she did the day-to-day things that must be done to sustain life. She set weirs, she cleaned and smoked fish, she mended clothes, gathered wood for her fire, kept her freshwater spring clean and grew to accept and even cherish solitude. And one day, busying herself at her work and knowing contentment because she had learned she could endure and survive by herself, Mowita looked up and from the forest came Copper Woman, her mother, back in new skin, back from her visit to her magical sisters, back from that source place across the path the sun makes when it sinks behind the water for its rest. And a gladness stirred in Mowita, for she was not alone. She ran to her mother and embraced her and they laughed and wept with joy. Some months later the gladness came forth and was twin girls, and one of them had green eyes, and thereafter, every so many years, Mowita carried happiness inside herself as a gift from the supernaturals and the Children of Happiness grew strong and their laughter echoed, and there was much music in their lives.

Children of Happiness are not like ordinary children. You can tell a Child of Happiness by the way she is different: she always seems like an old soul living in a new body. Her face is very serious until she smiles, and then the sun lights up the world. You look at the eyes of a Child of Happiness and you know the child knows everything that is truly important.

Children of Happiness always look not quite like other children. They have strong, straight legs and walk with purpose. They laugh as do all children, and they play as do all children, they talk child talk as do all children, but they are different, they are blessed, they are special, they are sacred.

They are to be cherished and protected,
even at the risk of your life.
They will know sadness, but will overcome it.
They will know alienation
for they see past and through this reality.
They will Endure where others cannot.
They will Survive where others cannot.
They know love
even when it is not shown to them.
They spend their lives trying to Communicate
the love they know.

The Children of Happiness had children of their own and Copper Woman grew old, spending her time with her grandchildren, teaching the girls the secrets of women, and this time even some of the boys could learn, for they were more complete than the sons of the incomplete Snot Boy, for Qolus/Mah Teg Yelah had proven, having been in his own time and place a wife, that in every woman dwell aspects of man, and in every man aspects of woman, so there is never any need for conflict.

Copper Woman knew her flesh was failing, interfering with her abilities, so she turned much of the responsibility over to

Mowita. When Copper Woman was so old even she could not remember how old, she became Old Woman. When Old Woman was so bent with age she could sweep the beach clean without having to reach down, she told Mowita it was again Time. Old Woman knew, and it was Time.

Her skin split, she again left her meat and bones on the beach, and she came from within, her Self freed. Mowita wept to know her mother was gone, and she wondered if she could survive and endure, and be and do all that Old Woman had been and done. She heard the daughter with the green eyes chanting the words to Old Woman, asking Old Woman to enter her, become her. Then the daughter with the green eyes, whose name is known only to the initiates, lay down on a bed of skins, and Old Woman, hidden in the skins, became pregnant. From this the green-eyed daughter lived as part of Old Woman, and lived in Old Woman, who was also part of and in her. And there are no easy answers to the questions that come with being told this; the answer lies within each of us, and each of us must find that answer for herself. Mowita knew then that it was not necessary for her to do all and be all that Old Woman had been and done, for the secrets were shared, and Old Woman was not Gone, only Changed, and would answer when needed. Mowita also knew that when it came close to her Time, there would be another to take her place, and when it came close to the Time of the green-eyed daughter, one would be recognized to replace her, and if.it was not known before the Time to pass over, it would be known after. But always the truth will be sustained and the secrets will endure, for Old Woman is watching, Old Woman is guarding, and with her all things are possible. When Mowita was Old Woman, she told the green-eyed daughter to prepare the rituals and be ready to continue as Old Woman, and to allow to come out of her that part of Old Woman that was in her. And always the disciples will aid the Old Woman and give her strength, the initiates will aid the disciples and the women will protect their Truth, glory in it and Endure.

And though all of this happened so long ago nobody can say when, still there are women who Know, and whether they are women who come from the lines of the black people, or from the lines of the brown people, or the yellow people or the white people, or whether they are of the line of happiness, still they may Know. And still, many are born but few are chosen. And still those who come with green eyes are held in esteem. Some are born, some come in search, and if they Know they are welcomed, so that within the Women's Society neither wealth nor social position counts, for these are imposed on earth by chance and whim, while within the society only that which grows from the core has any meaning.

When the Time came for the next change and the black-robed men moved to destroy the Society of Women, the women Endured. Not fighting, not disputing, clinging to their knowledge, they Endured, and now it is almost Time again, and much magic is preparing, and soon the sign will be known.

SISIUTL

There are those who think that only people have emotions like pride, fear and joy, but those who know will tell you all things are alive...

There are trees on the coast stripped of bark, stark silver white, and without the bark one can see how the very wood is twisted so the dead tree seems to be like a corkscrew rooted in the earth. There are those who think that only people have emotions like pride, fear and joy, but those who know will tell you all things are alive, perhaps not in the same way we are alive, but each in its own way, as it should be, for we are not all the same. And though different from us in shape and lifespan, different in Time and Knowing, yet are trees alive. And rocks, and water. And all know emotion.

There are rocks on the coast which, like the trees, seem corkscrewed, seem to twist upon themselves, as if in agony. Whirlpools and riptides are the same, only different. All because they have seen Sisiutl and tried to flee.

Sisiutl, the fearsome monster of the sea. Sisiutl who sees from front and back. Sisiutl the soul searcher. Sisiutl, whose familiars are often known as Stlalacum, the vision people, those who ride on the wind and bring dreams, the Stlalacum who search out the chosen and those who would see beyond the surface.

Sisiutl moves freely in water, whether salt or fresh, even in heavy rain, for he is able to transform himself. He seeks those who cannot control their fear, who do not have a Truth.

Fearful he is and terrifying. His eyes send cold fire into your belly and his forked serpent tongue flashes horror at your soul. No words can explain Sisiutl, who looks like a snake but has no tail, rather a head at both ends, each head more fearsome than the other, and from him emanates cold and horror.

When you see Sisiutl, you must stand and face him. Face the horror. Face the fear. If you break faith with what you Know, if you try to flee, Sisiutl will blow with both mouths at once and you will begin to spin. Not rooted in the earth as are the trees and rocks, not eternal as are the tides and currents, your corkscrew spinning will cause you to leave the earth, to wander forever, a lost soul, and your voice will be heard in the screaming winds of first autumn, sobbing, pleading, begging for release. Lost, no part of the Stlalacum who know Truth, no part of anything, alone, and lonely, and lost forever.

The bark flew from the frightened trees, leaving only the twisted wood exposed. Only the roots, deep in the earth, kept the trees from falling upward into the void.

When you see Sisiutl the terrifying, though you be frightened, stand firm. There is no shame in being frightened; only a fool would not be afraid of Sisiutl the horror. Stand firm, and if you know protective words, say them. First one head, then the other, will rise from the water. Closer. Closer.

Coming for your face, the ugly heads, closer, and the stench from the devouring mouths, and the cold, and the terror. Stand firm. Before the twin mouths of Sisiutl can fasten on your face and steal your soul, each head must turn toward you. When this happens, Sisiutl will see his own face.

Who sees the other half of Self, sees Truth.

Sisiutl spends eternity in search of Truth, in search of those who know Truth. When he sees his own face, his own other face, when he looks into his own eyes, he has found Truth.

He will bless you with his magic, he will go, and your Truth will be yours forever. Though at times it may be tested, even weakened, the magic of Sisiutl, his blessing, is that your Truth will endure.

And the sweet Stlalacum will visit you often, reminding you your Truth will be found behind your own eyes.

And you will not be alone again.

OLD WOMAN

And Copper Woman was tired. She felt there were other things for her to do, things she could not do in human form...

C opper Woman had been alive for many generations but had not changed. Her body was still strong and lithe, her skin had darkened to a rich brown in the sunlight, but her hair was still the colour of copper, and her eyes were still the green of the sea on a calm day, and her skin had only a few lines around the eyes and some lines around the mouth where she smiled often.

But she had been alive for many years. Her granddaughters were grandmothers now, and the children of the four sons of Mowita and the daughters of Copper Woman were many, and their children even more numerous. And Copper Woman was tired. She felt there were other things for her to do, things she could not do in human form, things she wanted to see that she could not see in her dugout, and so she talked to Mowita, her firstborn, and told her what she was thinking.

Mowita wept, but she knew the Time had come full. And she called for her daughter Hai Nai Yu, whose name means the

Wise One, or the One Who Knows, or several other things, and she talked to her, and Hai Nai Yu listened and went with her grandmother to the waiting house, and they sat on the moss and let the blood of the woman's time flow back to the earth and Copper Woman told Hai Nai Yu things she had not even told Mowita. Hai Nai Yu listened, and learned, and the wisdom was safe.

Then Copper Woman told Hai Nai Yu that the wisdom must always be passed on to women, and reminded her that whatever the colour of their skin, all people come from the same blood, and the blood is sacred. She said a time would come when the wisdom would nearly disappear, but it would never perish, and whenever it was needed, a way would be found to present it to the women, and they could then decide if they wanted to learn it or not. And Hai Nai Yu promised that when it came Time for her, she would be sure there was someone to replace her as the guardian of the wisdom, the keeper of the river of copper.

Copper Woman warned Hai Nai Yu that the world would change and that times might come when Knowing would not be the same as Doing. She told her that Trying would always be very important.

She left the waiting house for the last time, and she ate a last meal with her family. She held them all, kissed them all and reassured them she would always be there when there was Need.

She walked to the beach and sat by herself and waited until the sun was gone and the moon was high in the sky, painting the waves with silver. She stood then, and said the words, sang the songs, danced the dances and prayed the prayers.

Then she left her meat in her bag of skin, and took her bones with her, and became a spirit, became more than she had ever before been, more than any of us can ever be. She became Old Woman. She turned her bones into a broom and a loom.

With the loom she weaves the pattern of destiny.
With her broom she sweeps clean the beach
and the minds of all women who call on her.

She became part of fog mist and night wind
she became part of sea spray and waves
she became part of rain and storm
she became part of sunshine and clear sky.

She became part of night and part of day
she became part of winter and part of summer
she became part of spring and part of fall
she became part of all of creation.

With her loom and with her broom
with her love and with her patience
she weaves the pattern of destiny
and sweeps beaches and minds
she weaves the pattern of reality
and tidies shorelines and souls.

She will never abandon you.

TEM EYOS KI

She sang of a place so wondrous the minds of people could not even begin to imagine it...

Many generations after Old Woman freed herself from her meat and bag of skin, many years after the secrets began to be taught by and to the chosen women, the first period of testing occurred, a period Old Woman had known would occur.

The women for centuries had not concerned themselves with politics or argument. They left these things to the men, to give them something to occupy themselves with during the long, dark months of winter, when the weather does not allow fishing, hunting, whaling or food gathering. The women concerned themselves with spiritual things and with studying the teachings of the society, and with children, and keeping the society strong, and making sure life was lived as it ought to be, fully, with contentment.

The women became complacent. They thought because things had Always been so, they would Always remain so. And they did not notice that the men had begun to dominate many areas of society. Had become powerful. Had begun to believe their power was the way things were supposed to be.

Some of the women even thought the men were right, and that their ideas were as things were supposed to be. Slowly the men took control of society, took control of the government in the many villages, took control of all of life, until the women were left with freedom only within the Society of Women itself.

The men began to give orders to the women, and to say which man each daughter would marry. The men began to insist that inheritance should not come through the women at all, and that property would come under the control of the men.

Then, when things were not at all as they ought to be, a thing happened that is still spoken of among the women of the society.

Tem Eyos Ki went to the waiting house to pass her sacred time in a sacred place, sitting on moss and giving her inner blood to the Earth Mother. Men were not allowed near the waiting house, which was too sacred for them to understand or approach. Tem Eyos Ki stayed in the waiting house with some of the other women whose time it was, and she was there for more than four days.

When she came from the waiting house she was a woman hit by lightning, a woman struck by wonder, a woman shaken with power, a woman filled with love. She walked from the waiting house with a look on her face more potent than magic. Seeds of life glittered in her hair.

She smiled, and sang a song that told of love that knew no limits, of love that knew no bounds, of love that demanded nothing and expected nothing but fulfilled everything. She sang of knowing and trusting, of sharing and giving. She sang of a place so wondrous that the minds of people could not even begin to imagine it, a place without anger or fear, a place without loneliness or incompleteness.

She walked through the village singing her song, and the women followed her. They collected their children, boys and girls alike, and followed Tem Eyos Ki, leaving behind the cooking pots and weaving looms, leaving behind the husbands and fathers.

Tem Eyos Ki walked past the village, along the beach, toward the forest, singing her song of love and wonder. And the women followed.

The men found the village empty, the meals uncooked, the work unfinished. They followed the women, angry and threatening. They followed the women into the forest, followed the women who followed Tem Eyos Ki, who followed the song she had learned in the waiting house when she found love.

The storm wind tried to stop the men with gales and rain. The forest tried to stop them. Even the sky tried to stop them with thunder and lightning and the sea smashed herself against the rocks to warn the women.

The women wept and said they did not want to return home. The men threatened to kill Tem Eyos Ki, to silence her song so that she would never again tempt their women from their hearth fires. They went after Tem Eyos Ki to kill her.

But Qolus, who is a female figure and father of the four sons who fathered all ordinary people, sent a magic dugout, and Tem Eyos Ki leaped into it, still singing her song. She flew above the heads of the shouting men and the weeping women and sang of things people had forgotten. The storm stopped, the wind calmed, the rain stopped falling and the sea became still. All creation listened to the song of Tem Eyos Ki. Then she flew away.

The men stopped arguing and began to talk. The women said why they had wanted to leave. The men listened. The women listened. They went home together, to try to live properly again.

But sometimes a woman will think she hears a song, or thinks she remembers beautiful words, and she weeps a little for the beauty that she almost knew. Sometimes she dreams of a place that is not like this one. Sometimes she almost thinks she knows what it was Tem Eyos Ki was singing in her song. And she weeps for beauty she never knew.

FLICKER

When Tem Eyos Ki was pursued by those who wanted to kill her, she held her flicker feather close to her. The feather whispered to her and Tem Eyos Ki obeyed...

Flicker stitches the sky and holds it in place. Flicker swoops and rises, flaps her wings five times, swoops and rises again. Flicker comes to tell us when Bear is approaching, so that we can protect those women who are in their cycle, for the scent of a moontime woman can make bear forget everything except the hunger, the need.

When it is Time, and Flicker passes to the other after-life reality, she makes sure her body lies where we can find it so that we can honour it, then protect ourselves with what she herself no longer needs. Those who carry a flicker feather carry protection and magic.

When Tem Eyos Ki was pursued by those who wanted to kill her, she held her flicker feather close to her. The feather whispered to her and Tem Eyos Ki obeyed. She took her comb from her pocket, rubbed it with the feather, then threw the comb behind her. Immediately each tooth in the comb became a family of trees and a great forest put itself between her and those who would destroy her.

Tem Eyos Ki continued to flee and those who pursued her continued, forcing their way through the forest, calling for her death. The feather whispered to her again, and Tem Eyos Ki did what it said: she squatted and emptied her bladder, and an enormous river grew between her and her enemies.

The enemies used trees from the forest to make dugouts and rafts to carry them across the river, and Tem Eyos Ki could only flee again. The feather whispered and Tem Eyos Ki pulled out a handful of her own hair and threw it behind her. It grew, and spread, and became a stretch of bush, long grass and dry reeds, which ignited in the heat of the sun and put an enormous fire behind her.

And still the pursuers chased after her. The feather whispered and Tem Eyos Ki trusted what she was told. She gave herself over to Magic, and to the protection of Qolus and that most private and precious part of her body became a dugout, and she stood in front of it, singing of love, singing of faith, singing of truth, of freedom, and of trust, and was borne over the heads of those who would do her harm, was taken up, up to the other reality, singing, singing and safe from those who would kill her, singing and glorying in her song. And today every woman carries the proof, every woman carries her own dugout canoe, with Tem Eyos Ki standing in the front and singing, standing in the front and glorying, and at times of climax becoming, briefly, Old Woman, but only briefly.

THE WOMEN'S SOCIETY

And then the world turned upside down. Strange men arrived in dugouts with sails, dugouts that smelled terrible and were infested with sharp-faced, bright-eyed creatures the like of which had never been seen on the Island...

People were living almost as they were intended to live. Almost. And the Society of Women was strong. It was intertribal, open to all women, regardless of age, social status, political status or wealth.

No woman could buy her way into the society. No woman could inherit a position in the society. Each member of the society had been chosen by the society itself, and invited to join and become one of the sisters. Even slave women could belong to the society if they were invited, and their owners could not deny them the right to join, nor keep them from the meetings, nor forbid them to join in the ceremonies, for the society was powerful, and respected by all.

The education of all girl children was the duty of the members of the Women's Society. They taught with jokes and with songs, with legends and with examples. They taught the girls how to care for and enjoy their bodies, how to respect themselves and their bodily functions, and they explained to them all they would ever need to know about pregnancy, childbirth and child care.

And then the world turned upside down. Strange men arrived in dugouts with sails, dugouts that smelled terrible and were infested with sharp-faced, bright-eyed creatures the like of which had never been seen on the Island. These men wanted water and food, they wanted trees for masts, they wanted women, for it seemed as if they had none of their own. Their teeth were pitted and black, their breath smelled, their bodies were hairy, they never purified themselves with sweating and swimming, and they talked in loud voices. They wanted otter and seal skins and were willing to pay with things such as the people had never even dreamed of.

The world turned upside down. People got sick and died in ways they had never known. Children coughed until they bled from the lungs and died. Children choked on things that grew from the sickness in their throats. Children were covered with running sores and died vomiting black blood. Nobody was safe. Not the slaves, not the commoners, not the nobility, not the royalty. Entire villages died of sickness or killed each other in the madness that came from drinking the strange liquid that the foreigners gave for seal and otter skins.

And then new men arrived. Men who never talked to women, never ate with women, never slept with women, never laughed with women. Men who frowned on singing and dancing, on laughter and love. Men who claimed the Society of Women was a society of witches. "Thou shalt not suffer a witch to live," they insisted, but the people would not allow them to kill the women of the society.

Instead, the priests had to be content to take the girl children. Instead of being raised and educated by women who told them the truth about their bodies, the girls were taken from their villages and put in schools where they were taught to keep their breasts bound, to hide their arms and legs, never to look a brother openly in the eye but to look down at the ground as if ashamed of something. Instead of learning that once a month their bodies would become sacred, they were taught that their bodies would become filthy. Instead of going to the waiting house to meditate, pray, and celebrate the fullness of the moon and their own bodies, they were taught that they were sick and must bandage themselves and act as if they were not well. They were taught the waves and surgings of their bodies were sinful and must never be indulged or enjoyed.

By the time the girls were allowed home to their villages, their minds were so poisoned, their spirits so damaged, their souls so contaminated that they were not eligible to join the Society of Women.

The boys were taken away, too, and taught that women were filthy, sinful creatures who would tempt a man away from his true spiritual path. They were taught that women had no opinion that counted, no mind to be honoured, no purpose other than to serve men.

In less than a generation the world turned upside down, and reason and truth flowed out and were nearly lost.

The elder sisters died with tears in their eyes because the young women were not prepared to learn how to love their own bodies.

Who cannot love herSelf
cannot love anybody
who is ashamed of her body
is ashamed of all life

who finds dirt or filth in her body is lost
who cannot respect the gifts given
even before birth
can never respect anything fully.

The priests thought they had destroyed the matriarchy. They saw fighting and drunkenness where once there was love and respect. They saw men beating their wives and children. They saw mothers beating their children and even abandoning them. They saw girls who should have been clan mothers become prostitutes in the cities built by the invaders.

They did not see that a few women saved and protected the wisdom of the matriarchy, even at the risk of their lives. Meeting in secret, often in the churches of the invader, pretending to believe what the priests taught, being very careful of what they said, guarding jealously that which they knew.

Much was lost. Much will never be regained. We have only the shredded fragments of what was once a beautiful dance cape of learning. But torn as it is, fragmented as it is, it is still better than the ideas the invader brought with him.

A few women, old now, and no longer strong. A few elder women who kept alive what the invader tried to destroy. Grandmothers and aunts, mothers and sisters, who must be honoured and cherished and protected even at risk of your own life. Women who must be respected, at all times respected. Women who Know that which we must try to learn again. Women who provide a nucleus on which we must build again, women who will share with us if we ask them. Women who love us.

And there are young women now, some of them unlikely seeming candidates, who have been tested and found worthy, and who are learning the old wisdom. Young women who do not always manage to Do what they Know, and so need our love and help, our support and respect.

The dance cape is not complete, the song is not finished, the dance is not whole, the words are not all known. But the need is now and Old Woman is with us, and will help us and come to us when we most need her.

CHESTERMAN BEACH

"They came outta the fog, ships like nothin' we'd ever seen before, and then, like ducklings around their mother, boats and men pullin', comin' toward the beach wavin' and yellin' happily, as if the smoke from our houses was the nicest thing they'd seen in months..."

When I was a kid we'd sit around on the front steps in the evening, watching the fish boats, pleasure boats and yachts heading home, and listening to radios. Plural. What we did most nights was move the radio near an open window and sit outside where it was at least fresher, if no cooler, and then the other people moved to their steps with their radio near a window, and then some more people, and that way nobody had to crank up the sound to where it was a pain in the ear, and everyone could hear the news. Of course, if one dedicated individualist tuned in to a different station, that was kind of it for communication through sociability, but seeing as how we didn't have a whole lot of choice about stations, there wasn't much worry. At that time we got CBC or nothing. And CBC was often exactly the same as nothing, because the static wiped out the programs.

Now most of us have satellite dishes to bring in any number of channels, which doesn't mean we have unlimited choice in programming, because it seems as if most of these channels show the same programs, just at different times. How many *Seinfeld*s or Jerry Springers does the world need?

In the past years the salmon stocks on this coast have crashed; what used to seem like an endless bounty has become frighteningly scarce. Most of us have found the cost of gas and diesel more than can be made from the few fish caught, and have tied up our boats. Billy Peters, he'd even gone so far as to get four of the elders to stand on deck playing drums and chanting, the way they used to in the old days, and when that didn't do anything but give everybody a thrill and make the old men feel real good, a lot of the rest of us figured we might as well just sit 'er out, because when there's no fish out there, there's no fishing, either.

So the satellite dishes were bringing in nothing worth watching and we moved out to the steps, with the radio set by an open window the way we used to do all the time. Our neighbours saw what we were doing and with much laughing and teasing they did the same thing. And pretty soon most of us were sitting in the cooling air, watching the glory of a sky full of sunset and listening to the good old CBC, the fruity, over-trained tones of the announcer telling all listeners that the entire coast had been put on a red tide alert, and the taking of all clams, oysters and mussels was prohibited.

One of the boys snickered and said, "Red Tide. Hell, that's for the white boys," and a couple of others laughed and nodded, but my Granny shook her head and sucked her top teeth, then folded her hands in her lap. That's all she did. But Fred, he went into the house and shut off the radio, and Frank and Jackie and Jim came over from next door, so I went inside, got out the big enamel kettle and put it on the gas ring to boil for tea.

Angie Sam brought over a double batch of oatmeal cookies she'd just pulled from the oven and Alice and Big Bill brought a pan of brownies, and before the water was boiling, what with rolls and pies and buns and Christie's spice cake, and some other stuff that got mixed up elsewhere and then put in our oven to bake for later, well, we were set for a good old-fashioned evening. It felt so good I could hardly believe anything had ever interfered or that we'd ever been tempted to spend our evenings any other way.

Every bit as hard to believe was that my Granny said I should maybe take notes so I could write it all up later, so that then, for sure, the story wouldn't be lost when she died. For years my Granny has been matter-of-factly talking about when or after she dies, not because she's puny or sickly or morbid, but because for her and a lot of the old people, dying is as much a part of living as being born, and it's an important thing, a big step, and not to be taken lightly or left to chance or accident. But this was the first time she'd as good as told me to write stuff down. Usually I have to ask permission and lots of times she has said no, writing's for those too lazy to remember. Until I have permission, it wouldn't be right, so I've got a head full of stories. I got out my notebook, but mostly I used my ears, which is what I've sort of been trained to do by a lifetime of living and studying with her.

"We didn't call it Red Tide," Granny said softly, in English because so many of the young people don't speak the language well and others don't speak it at all.

We all sort of leaned forward to hear better and she told us the name in our language, but there's no use trying to write it down because you'd never be able to pronounce it anyway, besides which the alphabet doesn't fit the sounds of the language. We don't have our own alphabet, we never needed one, we had memorizers for the important things. Not all of us memorized everything, of course. Some people were interested and memorized family ties by birth and marriage, some memorized trade and fishing right agreements, some memorized songs, and chants for navigating by sea current, some memorized the words of songs or poems, or the steps of dances. Of course, that's a risky way to do it. Each smallpox or tuberculosis epidemic carried off whole chapters of what had been a real living history. But they told me at school the big library at Alexandria burned flat to the ground, so when it's time for rotten luck I guess it's just time for rotten luck and there's nothing any of us can do about it.

Red Tide is caused by little living things in the sea, plankton maybe, and it flourishes in sunlight and warmer water. The water off the island is never what you'd call warm, but everything is relative and summer is warmer than winter, and these little things multiply, and sometimes there's so many of them that they stain the water with the colour of their massed bodies. If oysters, clams or mussels strain this water through themselves and ingest these little things, well, it doesn't make them sick, but anybody eating them is going to get sick and probably die.

One time we went into Growler Cove and the entire little

bay was as red as raspberries. I stood on the deck, looking and marvelling. The water around the boat was like some kind of berry juice and the water beyond it was blue with long grey ribbons in it, like a piece of that cloth they call shot silk. And all around the cove the green of the trees, the brown of the trunks and the grey of the rocks, making me wish I had been given the skill to draw and paint pictures. I took some shots with my camera and they turned out well, really well, but nowhere near as stunning and spectacular as the reality.

"From the time all the salmonberries are ripe, past the time all the blackberries are picked, through the time of the oolichan run to the first frost," Granny half chanted, "nobody who wants to stay clean will eat of the female-appearing shellfish." If you don't know what Granny meant by female-appearing shellfish, well, take a good look for yourself sometime. Those milkweed pods are tame alongside a big blue mussel once she's been opened.

"Those who eat what is restricted may never suffer in this life, and nobody can say what price they'll pay in the next life, and it's not for us to know that. But many who break the religious food laws will die and there's no protection or cure. First a tinglin' in the fingertips, then around the lips and face. Tinglin' will become numbness. The numbness will spread and become paralysis. There is no pain. There are even soft sensations and brightly coloured dreams, but the soul slips away as the intoxication takes hold and then the breathin' stops and the body is a hollow shell. Just dead meat over bones, held together in a bag of skin."

There was a bit of silence, and then the young fellow who'd

said Red Tide was for the white boys took a deep breath and said, not looking at Granny, "I never knew anyone who died from it."

"I do," she said just as softly, and she whispered a few names and said some holy words. "A whole family: mother, father, five little kids. The parents were taken young and raised in residential school and never taught our ways. And they had a feed of clam chowder one night in the summer and in the mornin' when there was no sign of anyone, someone went over to check and they were all dead, and the leftover chowder sittin' in a bowl—white on the inside, blue on the outside— and we took the chowder, bowl and all, and buried it with the chowder pot she'd boiled it in, but it was too late.

"Used to be..." Granny accepted a cup of tea and the lemon tart Sammy Adams gave her, and after she'd blown on her tea to cool it a bit, eaten the tart and nodded her satisfaction, then rinsed her mouth by drinking the tea, she handed back the cup for a refill and started over again. "Used to be if there was a bay or cove full of redstain the news would get around pretty fast. Like if we spotted one here, we'd send message dugouts to Queens Cove, Zeballos, Nootka Island, Kyuquot, all our family tie villages, and we'd tell them. They'd send messages to other places, and then them places would warn others, and soon we'd all know. And maybe we'd mark the place with a carved warnin' board or post and for four years—four years without redstain—nobody would eat there. If there was a second bloom of it, we'd re-mark the place. We had people who checked the marked places regularly. If they said a place was clean, we'd go take down the carved post. But until they said there had been four full years without the redstain, that place stayed marked.

"But there were times the poison food was put to sacred use. Some of the things it was used for are still secret." We all nodded, respecting the secret, accepting the need for it to be a secret. "The old woman and some disciples would go and gather up a mess of infected shellfish and then they'd take 'em home and boil 'em up until most of the water was gone. And they'd dry and mash up the stuff, put the whole mess in the sun to evaporate, and what you'd have, after it was pounded good, was like a powder. And if you mixed it with water, well, you had poison."

She smiled a small satisfied smile to herself, and looked out over the water. "One'a Captain Cook's sailors died from redstain. Maybe more than one, but one for sure."

She sipped her second cup of tea and stared off past the houses to the beach, and beyond it to the ocean. She looked like someone who could see past that, to another time. More and more, now, she gets that look of See Beyond; she's been planning her death for so long I almost don't pay attention to her when she says something, but that look she's been getting is recent, and it says more to me, far more than anything anybody can say.

"They teach in school that Cook found this place. Well, he wasn't the first. He just got the credit because he was English and the English never did like to admit to bein' second to anyone. There were lots of strangers here first. And some of them were real friendly people. And others were not our friends. There were lots of Spaniards got here before Cook, a couple of generations before the English got here. The story is, it was part of their religion, sort of. They'd send out ships and crews lookin' for new worlds. Them that found somethin' got to report it to their king, and they became heroes. Them that didn't get back was angels or somethin'… what's that word for it, Ki-Ki?" and she said it in our own language.

"Martyr," I translated.

"Thank you," she smiled. Then, very uncharacteristically, she did a bit of bragging about me, which made me feel not just self-conscious and shy, but sad in a way, too, because she never did anything like that when she was vital. "This one," she laughed softly, "makes me feel as if all the years of my life have been well spent. Not just one language, this one has several languages, and can move from one to another the way we can move from one chair to the next."

"Besides which," Sammy added in a teasing voice, "she can play basketball and is hell in spikes on the soccer field."

"That too," Granny agreed. She drank more tea, then looked at the assortment of goodies on the table and grinned like a little girl at a party. "That lemon thing was very good." She looked at Sammy. "But it was kind of small," and she waited to see if he'd get the message. He did. He was out of his seat in a flash, getting a small plate, filling it with an assortment of goodies. He looked at me and I nodded; some of the elders can't eat much by way of dessert because of the diabetes thing, it's a real problem and probably a result of all those years in school living on food that ought to have been fed to a dog. Those kids would have cooked and eaten the dog, if there had been one. But they didn't get to scoop my Granny.

She and a few others were hidden from the cops and from everyone else who came here. One of the benefits of living on a little island, you have a chance to see who's coming at you long before they get to the wharf.

"Martyr." Granny said the word several times, as if the taste of it was sweet on her tongue. "Some of those martyrs came here." She giggled suddenly, her face sort of disappearing into all her wrinkles, and I could see the little girl she'd been a long time ago. The word that popped into my head is a goofy word, one that's been used the wrong way for too many years, but that seemed to fit the shadow-kid I had suddenly seen: perky. The word doesn't really fit my Granny. If I'd had time to think about it, I would choose words like "dignified" and "self-contained" and—and the word that filled my head was "perky." That's one of the reasons I love languages so much. Words aren't carved in stone; they're fluid and alive and you can use each of them in so many ways, just change the tone of voice and "dipper" is something you use to get water or it's a person so dim, so foolish and ridiculous, nothing but "dipper" will do to describe them. Or "goof." You can call someone a "goof" in almost a loving way, especially if you're laughing and teasing with a lover or a child. But change your tone and the look on your face and "goof" is as big an insult as you can deliver. "Perky" won out over any other word I could think of at the time, and I haven't tried to find a better one.

"We didn't get to see too many of the heroes," Granny said, handing her cup to Sammy. He went into the kitchen with it but he could still hear her voice: my Granny has a trained voice, not for singing but for talking, orating, which was considered to be *the* most important talent a person could have. She doesn't have to shout or even talk very loud, but her voice carries far better than the voice of someone who hasn't been trained. Sammy put water on to boil for tea, moving carefully so there wouldn't be any clink or clatter to interfere with what he was being honoured to hear.

"We got to see about three boatloads'a martyrs," and the dried-apple grin disappeared and the soft face of my grandmother hardened until it looked as if it had been carved out of stone, the unyielding stone of the granite cliffs. "Keestadores," she grated in a cold voice. "Keestadores, with metal on their bodies and metal hats on their heads, and no heart at all worth talkin' about," and we all sat still, feeling all kinds of things in the tone of her voice.

"They came outta the fog, ships like nothin' we'd ever seen before, and then, like ducklings around their mother, boats and men comin', pullin' toward the beach, wavin' and yellin' happily, as if the smoke from our houses was the nicest thing they'd seen in months. So we welcomed them. We even danced on the beach for them." And there was so much sadness when she said that, so much grief we all had to swallow and blink tears from our eyes. Dancing to welcome people isn't something we do lightly, it's a high honour and the way my Granny spoke, we knew the honour had been violated. "We even scattered waterfowl down on the water for them," she added. She shook her head in short, jerky movements, and we waited, not saying anything at all. Angie Sam handed my Granny a clean hanky, and my Granny took it, dabbed at her eyes, then at her mouth. "We welcomed them, fed them, gave them fresh water to take back to their mother ships, gave them baskets of food for their friends still on board. At first, things were okay, but bit by bit it started to get ugly. They had officers, and sailors, and soldiers, but the trouble came from their holy men, the priests in their robes." She said a word in our language. Those who didn't speak it looked to me for translation, but I couldn't get my throat and mouth to work together. The word meant "fanatic," and it meant insane and it meant dangerous and it meant poison, but not a clean poison like the red tide that had kicked off this evening session, it meant the kind of poison that bubbles out of a wound that's gone septic. I repeated the word my Granny had used and she looked at me as if I'd just surprised her by growing up in front of her eyes. She winked at me. The change in her face was amazing. It was like watching a mountain of flint just slip itself to bits. Even Angie Sam laughed softly.

Sammy came back out onto the porch with a full pot of tea in each hand. He had a fresh cup for my Granny, and that was the one he filled first. He handed it to her, and Sammy, who always manages to look like he's in the middle of a good joke and having a wonderful time, became, for the first time I could remember, formal and polite and so much like his grandfather, who my Granny says is one of the finest men who ever walked, that I was surprised. When he handed her the fresh cup of tea he spoke softly so that only she heard what he said. I know he said it in our own language, because my Granny reacted as if Sammy had given her something much more precious than a cup of tea. She waited until Sammy had poured for some of the others. Then, when he sat again, Granny nodded at him and continued.

"The priests had eyes like burning coals, and not even the memory of kindness in them. They started off complainin' about the kids swimmin' naked and wound up tryin' to control our lives. Wound up talkin' against the Women's Society, tellin' the men that women weren't supposed to be partners, weren't supposed to pass inheritance, were only there to be used by men, bossed around and traded like lifeless things. Seems as if everything about the women just stuck sideways in their throats. Don't know what their own women were like, never saw any of the Keestadore women, they only brought men and young boys who got used as women, whether they liked it or not.

"At first we shrugged, everyone does things different, but they didn't have the same attitude. Their Sunday-best manners wore off real quick, and next thing you know they pointed their big gun at a perfectly good tree and blew it up, just to prove what they could do. Gloria Bellis's house is where that tree was when it exploded like that. Her kitchen is just about over that place." She blinked a few times, clearing the old image from her eyes so that she could focus on the here and now. She sipped her tea and we all did the same. Then she ate a couple of bites of brownie, and nodded her appreciation. Sammy took out his tobacco and papers and rolled a smoke, then looked at Granny for permission to light it up. She nodded, and a few other people reached for their own smokes or makings.

"At first we shrugged, like I said before, but after the demonstration with the big gun, they got themselves on the prod. Said there'd have to be changes, real big ones, or they'd do to the village what they'd done to that poor tree. And inside'a no time at all, they were a real bother. Everything sort of went into layers, with the priests at the top, and a lot of what they were insistin' had to happen was altogether opposite what the lower-downs wanted. The soldiers and the sailors, even the officers might have been satisfied usin' the boys when there was no women around, but once they saw the women, that's what they wanted. Worse than mink." She sounded so disapproving that most of us grinned.

"No nobility or royal women would go near any of them, but some of the commoner women were willin' to trade personal favours for some of the strange things the Keestadores brought, and of course the slave women didn't have much by way of choice. The slave women didn't profit from the trade, but the people who owned them did. Mind you, there were families that just flat-out refused to order their slave women to go with the sailors and soldiers. Before long, the women who'd been with the Keestadores got sick. Real sick. Ugly sick."

Granny stopped talking for a long time. She sat holding her cup, staring out at the water where the first night shadows were walking on the waves, and we all sat and waited, knowing she was hurting, knowing she was remembering the shock and horror of the first encounter with syphilis and the murderous effect it had. Some of the women used the time to wipe sleepy faces and lay half-asleep little kids on my bed, where they popped thumbs in mouths and closed their eyes, feeling safe, knowing they'd get taken home when it was time. Some of us lit up those little green coils from Italy that keep the mosquitoes away, and I took Granny her shawl and made another big pot of tea. After a while we all settled down to hear some more of the history nobody ever puts into schoolbooks. We've heard the other side of the story so often, some of us even halfways believe it.

When Granny asked for her tea to be warmed up, we knew she was ready to go on, and we regrouped ourselves and watched the bay and the islands, as they are now and as they must have been all those years ago, before the logging companies came.

"One day the women called a meeting and said they didn't want no more Keestadores and no more interference or foolishness from them or their priests. And when the old woman told what the rottin' sickness was doin' to the women who'd been with the sailors, and described how ugly the whole business was, everyone agreed that hospitality might be one thing, but the lines have to be drawn someplace, and babies born without noses or with teeth all sharp-pointed like a cat's or a rat's is plenty of reason to draw the line.

"So the council met with the Keestadores and let it be known we'd had enough. None of the Keestadores had learned any of our language, but several of the memorizers had learned enough of theirs to get the message across. And they didn't like what they got told.

"We didn't cut 'em off from the water or tell 'em they couldn't fish no more, but we did put our village outta bounds. They objected, and for a while we had to make sure the Fighters were easiiy seen, with their big war clubs handy, and at first we moved all the mothers and children back into the bush in case they did the thing with the big guns they'd been threatenin' to do. We actually got quite a bit of help from the priests, once they knew the how and why of things and saw one of those damaged babies. They had some big meetin's and sermonized at the sailors and soldiers, and even showed them that poor awful mess of a baby. They gave it back to us, but they gave it back dead, its neck snapped. We took that as the first sign of decency they'd given us. The poor little thing was out of its miseries, and had gone back to spiritland and could heal the pain and fear it had felt here, get ready to come back again, try again in a better body.

"The Keestadores finally moved on a ways, and they didn't use their big guns, but they was still hangin' around and still a lot of trouble. They'd come as close as they dared to the village and try to smile and sweet-talk, and when that didn't work there were some dirty looks and some pushin' and shovin', and it got so's before we went to bathe and purify in the warm sulphur springs, we'd have to send twenty or thirty Fighters in to shift them others.

"One day we found one of the Fighters with half his head blown away and we knew the Keestadores done it, but we didn't know which one'a them, and we knew for sure by then they'd all lie about it and the one that done it would be protected by his friends and nothin' would come of makin' any fuss, and we figured maybe they'd just leave us alone now, worried that we'd let the priests know what had happened. Some of the other Fighters were real upset. A soul that dies unavenged don't rest easy, but mad as they were, they knew it just wasn't Time. You gotta wait until it's Time.

"Then one night we were all listenin' to a poet tell the new story about the sea and a make-believe trip to a magic land,

and we heard a god-awful scream. We all ran around tryin' to find out what it was, but all we found out for sure was there was two girls missin'. Little girls, ten and eleven. They'd been goin' to get the stuff for basket-makin'. One of them was learnin' how and wanted to show the other, and work on it while listenin' to the poet, and her friend had gone along with her to keep her company. But even though we looked all night, we didn't find 'em. Until first light. Then we found 'em."

She didn't raise her hand to wipe away the tears, she just let them flow down her face and fall to darken the front of her blue cotton dress. Her voice trembled but she just kept talking, almost chanting, and I figured she was keeping things inside a structure so she wouldn't just come apart with the pain of it.

"The first was found face down, floatin' half in, half out of the water, her legs bobbin' in the waves, her eyes open and starin' blind at the sand and rocks of the beach. Her dress was found later. Her body was covered with bruises an' bites, her little-girl breasts were scratched and chewed, but the sea had washed the blood away. A piece of cloth shoved in her mouth had stoppered her cries and there were blue fingermarks on her throat. But what had killed her was havin' the back of her head crushed, maybe by a rock, maybe by the handle of a Keestadore sword. She was dead when they chucked her in the water, but her last hours had been hell, and death come as a friend to her.

"The second was found in the bushes, lyin' on crushed salal, surrounded by huckleberry and Oregon grape. Naked. We never found her dress. They'd took their time with her and there was tears dried on her face, and places where the dust and dirt of her struggle was washed away by her cryin'. Her mouth was bruised, her lips cut and split and there was a big bruise on the right side of her face.

"The people had no way of understandin' what had happened. There'd never been anythin' like this in all the time since the beginning of life, and so they could only stare at the proof of horror and feel numb shock. They could see what had been done, but they couldn't understand how, or why. It had been hard enough to believe the Keestadores would force a grown woman to have sex when she didn't want, but the thought of sex with a child was too horrible for the people to even imagine, so they didn't know what to think. The old woman examined both the babies, and it was as if the sure evidence of what she found shook the centrepost of all creation, and threatened the here and now as well as the past and future, and she spent a long time alone in her sacred place, prayin' and askin' for help from the magic sources, help in understandin'. When she finally told us what she had learned from the prayers and magic, we believed her, but we still couldn't understand why anybody would want to do a thing like that.

"We didn't let the mothers of the girls near them until we'd washed and fixed them up, and nobody wanted to tell them what the old woman said had happened. Lots of us cried or was sick—or both—just thinkin' of what them babies had been through. Nobody wanted to think about it and nobody who knew could stop thinkin' about it, and everybody was... was just numb. Just numb.

"Some of the Fighters was all set to just wade in and let fly, but we cooled 'em down by pointin' out they'd never get 'em all and the survivors would still have them big guns, so we waited. Waited and never said a word. Never even told 'em two babies had gone over.

"The Keestadores had a camp down a fair piece from the village, with a boat out on the bay. They'd moved their horses offa the boat and had a fenced-off place for them at night but durin' the day they let 'em roam around pretty loose. There were guards posted at night to make sure nobody snuck up on 'em, and patrols durin' the day. They'd taken to bein' so fraidy and so tensed up we figured they'd gossiped with each other about what had happened to those babies, and were halfways expectin' trouble. None of us had said a word about it, but the way they behaved, movin' that far away, postin' the guards and all, made us suspicious. Well, we'd already been that, so it made us more suspicious.

"Some of the disciples and initiates met at the waitin' house and spent a time with Old Woman, prayin' and fastin' and meditatin'. And then half a dozen of them, sisters whose names are known only to the disciples and spoken only with love, went to the place where the Keestadores were. And one by one they chose a sentry and went walkin' up, smilin' as bold as you please, friendly and invitin'.

"You gotta remember, we didn't have no whores or floozies, these women were initiates of the Society of Women, students of Old Woman, like Ki-Ki is, proud of their bodies and knowin' they were clan mothers in the makin', and not one of 'em had been near a Spaniard that way before. Not one of 'em woulda gone near a Spaniard ordinarily.

"Them sentries thought sure they'd been blessed by their

god! They'd never known women raised to be proud of, and to enjoy, their bodies and all good feelin's. Inside of a couple of nights, guard duty was somethin' they was lookin' forward to, and the ones not on sentry duty would grin and feel jealous about each sound from the shadows. Rustlin' of grass and sighs and moans and sometimes a surprised yell endin' in the deep throat laughter of a teasin' woman.

"Well, the tide was low, real low, and that meant there was only one way in or out of the bay because a sand bar blocked the other way. There was an early fog rolled in after the sun went down and the ones on shore lit a big fire to push away the damp and the scary shadows.

"The dugouts came through the fog, movin' real quiet. Fighters from Tahsis, Kyuquot, Clayoquot, from Hesquiath, Yuquatl and Hecate, from villages that don't even exist any more because the epidemics killed 'em all. From Ehatisaht and Kelsemaht and Opitsaht and Kallicum. And don't judge by the numbers of people now—in those days there were a way more of us and we weren't just a buncha villages, we had a three-part confederacy, with our own navy, so to speak.

"Men and women pullin' the paddles, men and women who'd purified themselves and were ready to die or kill, men and women who'd faced their own fears and got past 'em and were ready now, if need be, to face the unknown of the other world.

"And on shore the sacred sisters walked out of the fog smilin', their bare breasts glistenin' with clarified seal oil, their skins perfumed with hemlock and bracken, their hair scented with the juice of flowers.

"Fog isn't solid like a wall, it blows and drifts, and where it's blown away the moonlight shines and the sentries seen the sisters movin' toward 'em and they started takin' off their metal helmets and the metal on their chests and backs, barin' their skin to the night air, to the touch of the sisters.

"The dugouts drifted in past the point and spread out in the fog bank, blockin' the passage. The women slid over the side, their bodies thick with whale oil against the cold of the water. Every fourth woman had a stone bowl full of burnin' coals, with a wet cedar basket over the top to hide the glow. The other three had seal bladders full of melted seal oil, or cedar pitch. Some of 'em had big chunksa blackpitch, which isn't always black but sometimes yellow, or golden, or even white. But it all burns somethin' fierce.

"The women swam real quiet up alongside the big wooden ship, and they started smearin' her all along and above the water line.

"The sacred sisters smiled and moved close to the sentries and let themselves be touched and stroked and coaxed into lyin' down on the ground. Them sentries got a real surprise when the sisters locked their legs around the sentries' waists and crossed their ankles behind the sentries' backs and fastened their mouths tight on the sentries' lips to smother all sound. Because then they used their knives to slit the Spanish throats.

"When the sentries quit thrashin' and twitchin', the sisters rolled out from under 'em and pulled on the Spanish helmets, breastplates and backplates, then stood in the wispin' fog, the blood, Spanish blood on their bodies, coolin' and dryin'. To the Spanish grouped around the fire, everythin' looked okay. The few little noises they'd heard only made 'em grin and wish they'd been on guard duty, and they couldn't see clear because of the fog and because they were so close to the big fire that their eyes couldn't focus in the dark anyway.

"The sisters made shrill whistle sounds, like skeeter hawks, and the army moved in from the woods, comin' quietly, slippin' from shadow to shadow, from fog trace to fog trace, keepin' rocks an' logs between them and the ones gathered around the fire listenin' to a musician playin' music from their home place. People from what's now Tofino an' Bamfield an' Ucluelet an' people of the Tse-Shaht who'd come down the canal, and people from just about everywhere around here. All the men and even some boys who hadn't quite finished their manhood trainin', and women who weren't pregnant or nursin' a child. Only the old ones, the young ones and women with little kids weren't ready to fight."

One of the fellows looked confused, so Granny quit talking and waited for him to either figure it out for himself or ask. He asked. "I didn't know women fought," he mumbled. "I thought just the guys—"

"Women fought." Granny sounded real patient and not at all put out about being interrupted. "Before the outlanders came, we didn't fight much at all, but when it did happen, all the able-bodied got into it. Except the ones who couldn't be harmed, the special or sacred ones like the dreamspeakers, or the memorizers, dancers, clowns, and women carryin' or nursin' life. Nobody would fight or kill any of them people because they didn't want their own in any danger. Kill a memorizer and you killed a whole hunka history, and if you're gonna kill someone's history, well, your own might not last long. And when that's gone, you just killed all your people who were here before you, all over again. Maybe even the only memory of yourself from a time before, so those people sat out any kind of fightin'.'"

"If a woman with a kid got killed, what happened to the kid?" Jackie asked, and we knew she was thinking about her own.

"The grandma took over, just like I done with Ki-Ki, or an auntie, or a family that was good with kids. All orphans were the responsibility of all the people, especially the chief and the rich, and lots of times the orphans were better off for wealth and status than if they'd never been orphaned. Nothin' can make up for not havin' a family, but everyone tried to make up for it as best they could."

It was getting nippy outside so we moved into the house and Granny set herself in her big old rocker and I put a bowl of milk down for the cat. We refilled the tea cups, put a hole in the cakes and cookies, and had a chat with each other. The mothers checked on the sleeping kids, and after a bit we all gathered around Granny again, some of us sitting on the floor, leaving the fold-out couch and the chairs for the old ones.

"When the army was in place, the leaders whistled, and waited. They'd set themselves in three bunches, so the Keestadores by the fire was surrounded, with the sea in front of 'em and angry people to the left, the right, and behind 'em, and that big fire blindin' them in the middle.

"And the swimmers, well, they heard the skeeter hawk whistles, and they put the glowin' coals into the oil and pitch on the wooden boat, and some of 'em got burned good doin' it, and then the stuff on the ship was burnin', and they started swimmin' for the dugouts. The Keestadores was yellin' and some of 'em was shootin', and one of the women swimmin' just gave a funny sound and went under the water. She was the first one killed—most of you here tonight are related to her or to her sister. She had two daughters who went to live with her mother after, and her sister had a big family, and the kids all grew up and got married and had kids who had kids that were old when I was a young girl.

"The Fighters in the dugouts let loose with lances with burnin' tips, or seal bladders fulla oil, or whalin' harpoons with burnin' bark lashed to 'em. The bladders'd hit the deck and spilled melted oil, and the lances or harpoons would set it on fire. A couple of the boys had stole some gunpowder and replaced it with sand so the Keestadores didn't know it was missin', and they put it in carved rattles, looked like wooden eggs with a handle, the two halves held together by strong lashin', with pieces of oil- or grease-soaked cloth stickin' out, and they had nails and sharp shells in there, too, and they fired 'em and flung 'em. Some didn't go off but the ones that did made a helluva noise, and a mess, too.

"And on shore they're runnin' around, pointin' and yellin', and they can see their ship has caught fire but they can't see the dugouts, and then the army came in on 'em, and it was awful. It was just awful.

"Some of the Keestadores on shore ran for their rowboats to either try to get away from what was happenin' on the beach or to try to help the ones on the burnin' boats, and they were just wiped out before they had a chance to even push the things in the water. And out on the chuck they managed to get a couple of boats into the water but they were no match for the dugouts and it didn't take long to sink 'em and kill all the Spanish in 'em.

"The horses bust out of their fenced-in place and ran up and down knockin' people over and steppin' on 'em and killin' Keestadores and us alike, and then one of 'em took off into the bush and the others followed, and for a long time after there were wild horses here and sometimes we'd catch one. They made good eatin', too.

"There were clubs whistlin' and swords flashin' and people screamin' and blood everywhere. And we saved the priests to the end, and gave 'em time to pray and then bashed in their heads.

"Not all of our dead got brought home to be buried. We had a ceremony on the beach for them taken, or washed away by the sea. When a soul dies in sin, or unavenged, it doesn't rest, it stays and haunts the place. And what was evil in life is evil after, so we hadda leave some others who'd been strong and good in life to run herd on the Keestadore ghosts. Sometimes at night you can see them on the beach, caught in a fight as has been goin' on for three hundred years, and there's some as can't sleep on Chesterman because part of their past is still fightin' there, and some as can't think straight while they're there, and others just feel real sad and don't know why.

"When we all got home, it still wasn't finished. The sisters who'd fooled the sentries had known before they did it that there was no chance they'd escape the rottin' sickness. We didn't have no way to cure it, and they knew that, too.

"They went to the house near the waitin' house and prayed. The Keestadore blood still stained their skins. And the people came to visit, but nobody touched 'em. We smiled, and sang, and shared time, but we never touched 'em. And Old Woman made her presence known and the old woman, she mixed up some of the redstain soup powder stuff and the sacred sisters drank it and got a bit affected. They laughed and made a couple of bad jokes, and lay down on their beds and drank more. And people kept talkin' and singin' and tellin' stories, and the sisters got dreamier and drank more of it, and soon we knew they were somewheres else, somewheres with bright colours and new music and good-feelin' air, and then, almost all at the same time, they crossed over and left their meat behind on their beds.

"Some of us was cryin' real bad. These shoulda been memorizers and teachers and mothers, and lived a long time. They were the best of us, and all of 'em dead. One dead on the beach from a bash on the backa the head, and the others from redstain.

"We picked up their beds so we wouldn't have to touch 'em, and took 'em to the beach and piled cedar logs and stuff, and lit 'em up, and sent their clothes and treasures with 'em. The one killed on the beach got brought back and burned, too, but not all of her soul come with her—part of it's still out on the beach. Night and day we fed the fire, and on the mornin' of the fourth day we let the fire die out, and that night, as the sun was goin' down, we all took baskets and filled 'em and took the ash to the sea and scattered it, and went back again and again, the songs and prayers and chants and speeches goin' until all the ash was scattered.

"And we remember their names even today."

Granny sat in her chair staring out at nothing, and we all got up and left her alone with the past and the sisters whose names are known only to those in the Society of Women.

THE LOST GOLD MINE

"Maybe it was because the Cowichan were so gentle, or maybe it's just that gold does that to people..."

The fog hid the sharp slopes of old Catface, closing in on us until you could hardly see the outlines of the house next door. The air felt grey and heavy, and people moved slowly or not at all, as if they, too, were grey and heavy, and their feet weighed too much to be lifted. I felt okay when I first woke up, but before long all I wanted to do was go back to bed, and for a while I did, but I only managed a short nap and then I was awake. I tried just lying there, but a bit of that and I felt as if my bones were starting to ache, so I got up again. In spite of the nap, even knowing I couldn't get back to sleep again, I felt weighed down, drained of energy, and wouldn't have been the least bit surprised to start sneezing or coughing or worse, like when you're coming down with flu.

Just before suppertime the wind started to blow with a vengeance. All the fog blew away and the rain came down on us, driving almost sideways, hitting the windows with a sound like handfuls of sand, seeping in under the doors and around the window frames while the screaming wind tried to take the cedar shakes off the roof and move them back into the forest where they'd been for two hundred years before they got cut.

We all wound up out in the mess, taking down the satellite dishes, wrestling them into sheds or to shelter behind the houses, tying them as flat and safe as possible. We'd lost enough of them to know that when the angry wind starts to blow, no cable, no rope, no nothing is going to keep the dishes in place, and anyway, even if some of it does remain fastened, the dishes themselves can come apart and bounce off, useless and ruined.

Without the dishes, reception was so bad that radio wasn't fit to listen to, just static and humming noises, and all the phones were on the fritz. We still had electricity and could have settled down to watch some videos. Lots of people, if not most of them, did just that. One by one they drifted over to our place to visit, bringing tea bags or ground coffee, or maybe cookies or fresh-baked bread, and we sat around for a while playing cards and talking, and some of the people worked on their knitting or their carving or whatever it was they did in their quiet times. Sammy Adams had his sharp knives and his chisels and he was working on a gorgeous piece of cedar, making a whorl for a spindle, but making more than that, turning the disk itself into a thing of beauty.

There was a time most of the houses had spinning wheels and most families did their own wool. Some had even tried for a while to raise sheep, but it didn't work out too well. There are too many dogs and they're always having pups, sometimes in places where you don't even find the litter until it's grown so big and so wild you'd be better off going after it with a three-oh-three than a bowl of food. That doesn't happen all the time, but often, and it's not something that anybody enjoys, but nobody here knows how to fix the females, and the closest vet is a one-hour boat trip away. We manage to use a sharp knife on most of the boy pups, but you know how it is, all it takes is one and you've got a crowd all over again. And if not dogs, bear. We don't know if we've got cougar or not. You never see them, which is why you won't find images of them in our artwork—they were so crafty and so sneaky there were people who didn't think they were real, but rather some kind of evil spirit, just big eyes glowing in the dark or a hint of shadow half seen between trees. It's hard to tell what a thing looks like if you never see it. We knew there was something out there, but the truth is there are *lots* of somethings out there. The sheep didn't have a chance, and people went back to buying sacks of fleece. The more you were willing to do yourself, the less the fleece cost, so there were bags of smelly wool in just about every house, and in the evenings people talked and joked and carded and spun. And, of course, knit. A couple of women did weaving, but mostly not, unless there was something special they wanted made. My own thought on it is that weaving isn't really a very companionable thing to do. It requires concentration and counting, and it's really more of a daytime thing, like a regular job of work, and with kids running in and out and wanting this and that, daytime wasn't restful enough for a person to get deeply into the job. So mostly it was knitting. I've seen many a woman sitting with a big ball of wool on her lap, needles in her hands, her eyes turned to the TV and her fingers still busy. Annie Cameron has been known to take her knitting with her to the movie house in town and sit watching a techni-colour musical while finishing off whatever project she was working on. One time she watched *Gone With the Wind* two times, one after the other, and still managed to turn out the back of a diamond-patterned vest.

Granny was working on a cedar basket, her bucket of water on the floor by her feet, the cedar strands soaking so they would stay pliable. Her old hands are wrinkled now, and the knuckles are swollen and knotted, but she still makes the best baskets on the coast—so fine and tight and even, the designs showing clear and sharp. There are stores in the city willing to buy the baskets any time she sends them down, and they pay top dollar without arguing. Mind you, if you should drop by one of those stores you might see the baskets for sale at three times what they paid Granny, but that's how those places do things. Once we found out for sure about the huge price increase, Granny stopped sending down big boxes with a dozen or so baskets stacked inside and started stockpiling them for the summertime when the tourists arrive here. A lot of them are a total pain in a very private place, especially the ones in kayaks. They head off with maybe a two-day supply of granola and ichiban noodles, a frying pan and plenty of coffee and a pot to make it in, and stay out for a couple of weeks, feeding their faces on rustled stuff from the oyster and clam leases. About the only thing they leave behind are piles of their own shit with coloured toilet paper flapping in the wind. It's hard to feel welcoming when you know people are behaving like that. Then there's the ones come in the bigger boats, they raid the oyster and clam leases, too, and empty their holding tanks just offshore so it bobs in on the next tide, more toilet paper and even tampons and condoms. How to leave your mark, I guess.

The government is always going on about eco-tourism. I don't see much future in it. Not unless the ones who come supposedly to appreciate the beauties of the coast learn how to keep their crap to themselves. And how to keep their touchy-feely fingers off the shellfish leases. But they seem to think they're doing us a huge favour. One guy, when told he was stealing other people's oysters and leaving a mess, got real indignant. Well, he says, I travelled all the way from Montreal to learn about your culture. No, said Fred, you travelled clear across the country to make a damn fool of yourself.

When Granny started to tell her story, she didn't look at any of us. She kept her eyes on her work and let the words fall softly into the quiet. We didn't have to listen, she wasn't trying to teach us anything, she was just offering a story for anybody who wanted to listen. Sometimes strangers get uneasy talking to my Granny, because she doesn't always look directly at them when she talks. When Granny looks at you, she fixes you with her deep black eyes until you feel like she's looking right into the inside of your head, but it isn't always polite to do that, it doesn't leave a person much privacy, and there are times we find it impolite to force even our gaze on someone. Also, Granny doesn't always look at you when you talk to her, so sometimes people who aren't from here think she hasn't heard them. But there isn't much goes on around her that my Granny misses. It's just that she uses her ears to listen, not her eyes, so she doesn't have to look at you, she looks off at something else, or watches her hands, or maybe sits nodding at the floor, listening and giving you all the room you need to express yourself.

We sat where we felt most comfortable, letting the wind scream at the roof and tug at the door. Once in a while someone would get up quietly and add another piece of alder to the fire in the big black stove with the worn nickel designs. When it's warm we have a gas ring for heating water or cooking, and there are full bottles of gas come in on the freight boat regularly, so we don't have to worry about running out of gas. But when it's cold or damp, like it is all winter and part of the autumn, we light a fire in the wood-burning stove, and there's always lots of alder for fuel. Alder may be the biggest and fastest growing weed on the coast, and we make jokes that the funny sounds we hear at night are the sounds of the alder trees growing. The crackling of the fire in the stove made a peaceful sound that sometimes filled in the pauses between words as Granny wove her basket, and her story, which probably won't ever get into the history books in the schools and only survived for us to hear because other people, before my Granny was born, memorized it and told it to their students, who memorized it and told it to younger people. It takes years and years of training and practice to be a memorizer and I didn't always live with Granny, so I've got a lot of catching up to do. And like I said before, Granny is very aware of her time running out and I think she finally realized I wasn't going to learn and memorize enough stuff so she gave permission for it to be put to paper. Which is a *huge* concession on her part, because anytime something is the first time, it's scary. And not to be done lightly.

"Just about the same time the people up-coast were introduced to the Keestadores, the people down-coast met up with 'em, too. Now, there's some people say we're a hard-nosed and belligerent bunch, but them as aren't part of us are always jealous of us who are, and their opinion doesn't count for much anyway. We're the singers, the Kwagewlth are the carvers, the Salish are the politicians. And the Cowichan are the philosophers. Real gentle people, most of the time, always able to look at two or three or all sides of a question and always willin' to study with and share ideas and stories with other people. They've got the reputation for the most poetic language on the coast, but I don't know because I don't speak any of it or understand it spoken to me. But John, now, he speaks plenty of languages and he said speaking Cowichan was like carrying on a conversation in pure poetry, and I have no doubt he told the truth.

"Maybe it was because the Cowichan were so gentle, or maybe it's just that gold does that to people. We had a lot of gold here but we never mentioned it, not to keep it a secret but because we didn't think it was good for anythin'. It won't hold a cuttin' edge, and there was more of it than there was of natural copper, so we figured the copper was the precious metal, and used it for jewellery and ornaments. Maybe the Cowichan thought the Keestadores, who seemed to know a lot about metal, might know what to do with the stuff, so they showed it to them and asked what it was good for, which makes me wonder about havin' a mind that always looks for new ideas. In no time at all the Cowichan were faced with a choice of slavin' in a gold mine or bein' dead from a Spanish sword.

"They cut and blasted a big hole in the mountain and started whippin' and beatin' people to get 'em to haul out rocks and gold. Men, women, and all but the little bitty kids or the very old were workin', and the ones not workin' were penned up in the middle of the village and held hostage. Anyone did anythin' wrong, they got beat and the hostages got abused. A person might take a beatin' for herself and consider it worth it, but when you know your sister or some little kid is gonna get beat if you don't behave, you think twice about tryin' anythin'.

"A couple of people tried to get away and let other tribes know what was goin' on, but what happened was so awful, and the small and the old suffered so much, they all decided it wasn't worth it, so the Keestadores had it pretty much their own way.

"There was a girl had been livin' with the Tse-Shaht, learnin' how their women caught babies and teachin' the Salish weavin' she'd learned from someone else, and she was on her way home when she noticed this big mess on the hill. She didn't feel good about it, and the Cowichan, they always respect their feelin's, so she got the pullers takin' her home in the dugout to pull into a small crick and stay outta sight for a while, and she snuck close and just let her eyes find out the story. She seen the Keestadores whippin' at people and takin' them up the path to the mess, and she seen how wore out the ones comin' back were, and she went back and got the pullers to turn around and take her back up-coast, fast.

"The Tse-Shaht, like the rest of us, had just found out about the two little girls when she got back, and everyone believed what she had to say. When the Chesterman thing was done and the sacred sisters honoured, the whole fleet headed south.

"On the way down, other bands and tribes joined. There were fast two-and four-puller sealin' dugouts goin' on ahead to tell the people that the fleet wasn't just on a raidin' party or tryin' to invade anyone's fishin' territory. As soon as they said why it was headin' down, people joined in, either because they liked the Cowichan or because they figured maybe they'd be next. And, too, I guess it's true some people just like a good fight. And probably they like it because they're so good at it!

"Halfway down, the sealers came racin' back to say there was a Keestadore boat headin' up, and the fleet hid itself and had a long talk about whether to try to take 'em now or later. At first everyone was so steamed up they were all for now, but then they figured there was sure to be some noise, and people would get hurt or killed, and they needed all the Fighters they could get because gettin' the Cowichan out from under was the important thing. So they just lay quiet and let the big galleon go by, and they planned plans and dreamed dreams for later.

"They hid the dugouts again a mornin's easy walk from the village, and they snuck in real close and just watched. They saw the Cowichan taken up the mountain path, and they saw the others brought down, wore out and some with marks from the whips, and they planned, and figured, and prayed, and waited.

"That night they hid themselves on either side'a the path goin' up to the mess and when the Cowichan was brought up in the mornin', all the Fighters were ready. A Keestadore officer up front, and Keestadore guards along the file, and another officer bringin' up the rear. There'd be five or six or maybe ten Cowichan, and then a Keestadore with a whip slappin' at them, and then some more Cowichan, and another Spaniard, and like that, all the way down the line.

"When the whole bunch had gone past the woman at the foot of the hill, why, she stepped out real quiet. She knew there was no sense tryin' for the head because'a the helmet, and the back and chest was covered with armour, so she just grabbed the officer by his bearded chin, lifted his head and slit his throat before he could even gurgle, let alone yell.

"Of course the Cowichan weren't goin' to raise the alarm. They just kept walkin' up the mountain, actin' just like they always did, makin' sure she was hid from sight while she put on the Keestadore armour and took his place. If the officer at the front had turned around, all he'd'a seen would have been the metal hat glintin' in the early mornin' sun, just like always.

"The next Spaniard in front of her, he got the same treatment when another Fighter stepped out of the bush, real quiet, and did the same thing to him. The second Fighter, he was a Sne-Ney-Mo, and you know what kind of chest, shoulders and arm muscles they have. When he slashed, he near took off the entire head and he said later it was all he could do not to give a big whoop of triumph. But he held it in, and pulled on the blood-drenched metal armour. One by one, workin' from back to front, they slit the Spanish throats, put on the armour and pushed the dead bodies out of sight. When the officer looked around, everythin' looked just the same to him as it was supposed to, right up until his own chin was grabbed and the last thing he saw was his own blood spurtin'.

"The Cowichan knew where he kept his key, and how to use it to unlock the chains around them, and they did that, but didn't take 'em right off—they wanted to arrive lookin' as close to normal as they could. They all hid knives and such that the Confederacy Fighters give to 'em, and when they got to the mess at the top of the path, they shuffled and kept their heads bent and looked at the ground same as always, and the Spanish guards moved forward to change wore-out workers for fresh ones and it was all over in no time flat. All the Spaniards were dead, and their bodies all thrown in the hole in the hill.

"The rest of the Cowichan were unchained, and the Keestadore swords an' armour were divided up, and everyone trooped almost all the way back down to the village again. They stopped and re-formed a pretend column of Cowichan. They had chains around 'em but they weren't locked shut, and everyone had a knife and plenty of reason to use it.

"One of the Cowichan chiefs snuck carefully down to his own house and went inside and got his family war club from where he'd hid it where the Keestadores wouldn't find it. He'd got it from his mother's oldest brother, who'd got it from *his* mother's oldest brother, and it was somethin' every Fighter envied. It was as long as a tall man's arm and so heavy only the strongest men could lift it, and it looked mean. It had been part of the root of an old arbutus tree, and there was a big rock in the end of it where the root had grown around it in the ground, a hundred years before it was undercut by a creek and toppled over with the roots pulled up out of the earth by the weight of the tree. The rock was as big as two fists clenched together, and all around it, set into the wood, were whales' teeth and pieces of walrus tusk, so it crushed and stabbed and cut all at the same time. When he swung it, the wind swished between the rock and the wood, between the teeth and the tusks, and it screamed like an eagle does sometimes.

"The Confederacy Fighters and the freed Cowichan were right in the middle of the village when the Cowichan Chief came outta his house with his club held up, and he swung it, and it screamed for him and then he let out the most godawful yell, and the fight was on and it was here-we-go time.

"Some of the Keestadores tried to get their boat underway but it takes a long time to get the sails up and they didn't have all the pullers they needed for the long oars that stuck out the sides and down to the water. They tried to make a fight of it with the big guns, but the dugouts were already too close. Some of the Fighters had stayed back with the dugouts and were waitin' just out of sight around the point, and when the yellin' and fightin' started, the navy came in at full speed, every puller sweatin' and keepin' the rhythm just exactly. They got in so close to the big wooden ships that the Spanish couldn't point the guns down enough—they fired right over the heads of the pullers and into the sea. The firelances did it to the sails, and then they just hitched cedar bark ropes to the big boat and steered her onto the rocks and let the sea do most of the work for them.

"The sailors and Keestadores on the wooden ship had to swim for it, but they didn't have a chance. The dugouts closed in on them one at a time, and the steersman or steerswoman just leaned over and bashed in the heads of the swimmers or sent a whalin' harpoon through 'em.

"They took the Keestadore dead up to the mine and tossed 'em inside, and then let the priests go in and pray over the dead. And while the blackrobes were prayin', the Confederacy used Keestadore powder to bring the hill down over the hole, buryin' the whole lot of 'em in with the gold they'd wanted so much.

"But then they saw how raw the earth looked there, and they knew it would be easy to tell there was Somethin' there, and it wouldn't take much figurin' to know what, so they got the idea to hide the evidence and suck in that other Keestadore boat at the same time, and they lit fire to the bush.

"Some of the holy people were upset about that because cedar and hemlock are sacred and arbutus is blessed and balsam is holy, and destruction is a sin, but when people have smelled a lot of blood, their brains go funny, and they lit the bush.

"Between the blast that sealed the mine and the smoke from the bush fire, the other Spanish boat came back in a rush. From where they were it musta looked like the Keestadores was chasin' the Cowichan for water and stuff to fight the fire. They could see the other boat bust on the rocks, and of course they wanted to help, and with their attention turned to two wrong directions, they didn't see the navy dugouts until they were up close, and the big guns were no use again.

"It wasn't as easy to get the last big boat because the sails were already up, but they threw bladders of oil through the holes where the oars stuck out, and sent fire arrows and lances in and started some small fires. Some of the dugouts were sunk this time, and the big wooden ship just rode right over 'em, splittin' the cedar and crushin' and drownin' men and women.

There were so many dugouts, and so many Fighters, and the fires were spreadin' and the sails were startin' to burn and the ship didn't have much room to manoeuvre in the bay, and the smoke from the fire was makin' it hard to tell what was goin' on. Some of them Sne-Ney-Mos had found more of that powder, and they talked to some Cowichan about the stuff and then crammed 'er into some of the floats they used to keep seals from sinkin' after they've been speared. They used 'em the same way we'd sent in the oil and set it afire. They didn't go off with a huge crashin' boom—I guess there's more to makin' a bomb than that—but they did add to the noise and they really set the fires to burnin', so they chucked a few more of 'em up on the deck, as well.

"Finally it was the same as before, the boat burnin' and people tryin' to swim to safety and not findin' any safe place, swimmin' in water red with blood, hearin' the chant of the paddlers comin' closer, and then not seein' anythin' at all, and all of 'em died.

"Before anyone got to celebratin', the wind shifted and the Cowichan and the Confederacy had to get away or burn like the bush they'd set afire. They headed north in dugouts, and it was like the bush wanted vengeance. The fire crowned and chased after 'em, sometimes missin' entire stands of timber, like around Nitinat, fed by the wind, leapin' from the top'a one tree to the top'a another, faster than a swift runner, and the heat so hot some of the small lakes boiled like pots on the stove and people who'd tried to find safety in them died of hot water and no air to breathe.

"Before it was over, a third of the island had been burned, a lot of people were dead or homeless, and innocent animals who'd had nothin' to do with any of it were gone forever."

Granny put her basket work aside and got up from the sofa and walked to the bathroom. We made a pot of tea and waited for her to come out and tell us some more. But when she finally came out of the bathroom, she didn't look at us or speak to us, she just went into her bedroom and closed the door. So we finished our tea, washed the cups and left them to dry on the counter. Then everyone else went home and I went to bed to listen to the wind howlin' and the rain splashin', and to think about what it must have been like long before my Granny's granny was born.

KLIN OTTO

"There was a song for goin' to China and a song for goin' to Japan, a song for the big island and a song for the smaller one. All she had to know was the song and she knew where she was..."

We were sitting on the deck of Mabel Joe's fish boat, leaning against anything we could find to lean on, the summer sun almost too warm on our faces, the wind blowing our hair and tugging gently at our clothes. Shaula's little girl Trina was sprawled on her blanket, sound asleep in the shade of Big Bill's shirt. It was a Hawaiian shirt, with bright green palm trees with red-brown trunks against a red and yellow sky, and it billowed and flapped above her. Peter, Big Bill's different-looking son, got him the shirt from a bin in the St. Vincent de Paul store in Vancouver when he took his rabbits over to win all the prizes at the Pacific Exhibition, and while I personally figured it to be the ugliest shirt I'd ever seen, Big Bill wore it on every possible occasion. Alice teased him sometimes about even sleeping in it, and he'd just laugh and put his arm around her and give her a bit of a squeeze and laugh again and say, "Well, if I do, you're the only one knows for sure," and then they'd give each other a quiet special little smile and anybody watching would smile too, from them being so happy. There's people hook up together and everything's real nice between 'em for a while, then it's gone, and it's as if they're bored with each other or they get to be resentful and nasty. But Big Bill and Alice treat each other as if each one of them thinks the other is the very best piece of news since the dawn of time.

My Granny was sitting on the fish box, her legs dangling down like a little kid on a too-big chair, swinging her legs slightly, tapping one foot rhythmically, her face soft, eyes dreamy, lips moving, making silent words only she could hear.

The soft steady sound of the engine drifted through the snatches of conversation like a tune on a radio nobody was listening to, and behind us the white wake from the twin screws bubbled up from the blue water and trailed back to the village like a path. Mabel used to fish full-time and she did real well at it. The old people said it was because she fished by the old rules and followed the teaching of Big House.

Mabel should have an entire book written about her. Nobody knows where she comes from, not even her mom and dad. They found her after a big storm, lashed into a life jacket, held in place with just about enough duct tape to waterproof a submarine. She's definitely First Nations, but nobody has a clue which bunch of us—she might be from any nation. They have a good idea how old she is because of the number of teeth she had when she was found, but other than that her origins are, as they say, a mystery. And she didn't go to residential school because they hid her. That happened a fair bit, actually, and it wasn't easy to do what with RCMP dropping by to, they said, just say hello, and then there's Fisheries and Wildlife, and this religious person or that one coming to do missionary work, and all of them more than willing to report any school-age kid they see.

Mabel grew up pretty much the old way, except for the ways the modern living intrudes, even in the isolated coves and bays. Things like the Mickey Mouse radio and going to town for groceries and catching a movie or two while you're there. And inoculation and dentist and stuff like that.

When she was, oh, sixteen or so, her dad had a stroke. Made a sort of choking sound and fell to the deck of the wharf. We all burned smudge and said words of thank you that he'd been tied up at the time, because if it had happened when he was out on the chuck, well, that might have been the end of it. But he went down not seven feet from a fish buyer. And again, it was burn smudge and say thank you because the fish buyer had his St. John's Ambulance industrial first aid certificate. He called for an ambulance and went with it to the hospital and was human person enough to come to the village to tell us what had happened and where Mabel's dad was. He even took Mabel and her mom back with him. Mabel's mom stayed with some cousins so she could go up and see her husband every day, and help with the physiotherapy and that.

And Mabel, she took the boat out and continued with the fishing. Of course the Fisheries and the Mounties and a few others finally got themselves into it and told her that *she* didn't own the licence on the boat so she wasn't supposed to fish, only her dad could. By then her dad was ready to leave the hospital so Mabel just went and got him, and set him in a chair on deck. There, she says, he's on-board and he's going fishing. Excuse me all to hell. She took her mom with her, too, because she had been watching the physio and she knew what to do. And out they went. Bit by bit they got the money together, or at least made it look as if they had got the money together, for Mabel to buy the boat and the licence. When that was in place, and all the legalities tickety-boo, Mabel's mom and dad stayed home and she just kept on fishing, supporting the family.

When the fish stocks began to crash, Mabel was one of the first to take advantage of the government buyback scheme. She used a bit of the money to do a changeover on the fish boat, and now she takes tourists out on what they call charters. She makes sure they have their sport fishing licences and all the permits are in order, and she takes them out for as long as they're willing to pay. They sleep on board, she cooks, and she takes them to all these places they'd never get a chance to see otherwise, old village sites and hot springs where they can soak away the tension and stress of their regular lives, she takes them hiking up bluffs and shows them some of the stuff that was here before the last ice age, shows them stuff that survived and that they probably would never get a chance to see without her. She gets a lot of repeat business—after a week with her, people go back and return to their life, and right away they start to squirrel away money so that the next trip they take can be longer. There's one guy, he's a doctor who comes every year for a month, and he could probably hire Mabel exclusively, but he doesn't mind if other people pay and go along, too. Lots of times they stop at places where someone isn't feeling well and the doctor, he looks after them free of charge. He says when he retires he's moving here full time. The last time he came for a trip, Mabel didn't even charge him.

When it isn't tourist time, Mabel takes older people into town, to do what they need to do there. They'll call up on the Mickey Mouse and she'll go to wherever it is they live and fetch them and head down to town for shopping, or doctor, or even a hospital stay, or whatever. Several times she's taken women in to hospital to have their babies and wound up doing the catching herself, and one of the babies is called Mabel, and another is called Joe. Not Joseph, just Joe. She's never been involved seriously with anybody, says she doesn't have time, she's too busy to be able to do somersaults or back flips or anything else that needs her to be head over heels. If she ever slows down enough to begin to think about it, she's going to make someone think they've been hit by a freight truck.

My Granny started singing, an old song from the days before fish boats and engines, from before compasses and printed charts, from before the strangers came out of the fog and things began to change. Mabel sang along with her and Granny smiled at her, and the two of them almost shone with the sharing of the words the rest of us had never heard before. Those of us who knew the first language heard the names of places we'd never seen, descriptions of bays and coves, headlands and constellations, rivers and beaches, coves and fjords. We all sat silent, and in spite of the warm day, there were goose bumps on my arms and legs. Then Granny quit singing and started talking, her voice rippling like water, her eyes fixed on something nobody else, not even Mabel, could see.

"They were fair-skinned people with supernatural powers who had the ability to levitate," Granny said in her own language, "and they brought us the ceremonies of absolution and ecstatic revelation."

Then she smiled and focussed her eyes on some of the young people who don't speak the language, and she switched to English, some of the rippling water sound disappearing from her voice.

"Copper Woman was livin' alone when the magic people came from the skies, down the path the sun makes on the water, comin' in a dugout like nothin' any of us has ever seen. They stepped out of it but didn't touch ground, they floated like fireweed fluff until they got to where she was standin', starin', nearly shakin' with fear, and then they settled to the ground, soft and gentle.

"She'd been alone a long time, she'd been lonely so long she had forgotten there was any other way to be, but she'd remembered what she knew and tried to stay strong inside.

"She showed the magic women the house she'd built with rocks and logs, near the fresh-water stream where the fish came up to spawn in the pools, and she cooked food for them and never even wondered how they knew her language.

"They stayed with her, ate with her, fished and swam and danced with her, and they taught her things she needed to know."

Granny started to sing again, and though I had heard the song before, I didn't know how to interpret the words.

"She told them she'd never gone far because she wasn't sure she'd make her way back again, and they taught her a song and a rhythm, and told her this place was safe for her, and she'd never be lost again, and they went with her in the dugout made from a livin' tree, and introduced her to magic. They introduced her to Klin Otto.

"Klin Otto is a river in the ocean, a current of salt water that starts in one special place off a bay in California and runs in a set pattern up to one special island in the Aleutians. And Klin Otto, she never changes speed, and she never changes direction, and she's always there, now until forever. The life-span of a woman is 80 years; there have been 187½ lifespans since Klin Otto was revealed to Copper Woman, so you know that since Old Woman was grown at that time, she is now 15,000 years old, and that's how long we've been on this coast."

She sang some more, and we listened. The baby slept, her index finger in her mouth, and the silly clown puffins fell over themselves to get away from the fish boat. Or they pretended to, because however much splashing and flapping they did, they never really went *away* from us.

"Everythin' we ever knew about the movement of the sea was preserved in the verses of a song. For thousands of years we went where we wanted and came home safe, because of the song. On clear nights we had the stars to guide us, and in the fog we had the streams and creeks of the sea, the streams and creeks that flow into and become Klin Otto.

"The steerswoman or steersman stood at the front of the dugout and tapped the beat of the song with her stick against the carved prow, and the pullers pulled to the rhythm, all at once, so many pulls on one side. Then they'd all switch at once and the paddles would hang in midair for a beat, then dig in on the other side, all together, all pullin', and the steerswoman singin'. When she wanted to know exactly where she was, even in fog or rain when you couldn't see the stars, she'd be able to figure it out. She had a rope made of sinew that was woven and braided together a special way, and knots were woven into it at regular spaces. The rope was attached to an inflated seal bladder of a special size and weight. The pullers would stop pullin', the dugout would move at the speed of the current and, still singin', the steerswoman would wait for a special line in the song, then she'd throw the bladder into the sea and count the knots as they passed through her fingers. That told her how fast the dugout was goin'.

"When she knew the speed of the current, plus how fast the pullers had been pullin', she could figure out in a minute where she was by the line she was singin' in the song.

"There was a song for goin' to China and a song for goin' to Japan, a song for the big island and a song for the smaller one. All she had to know was the song and she knew where she was. To get back, she just sang the song in reverse.

"The words of the songs and the words of the purifyin' ceremonies and the meanin' of the chants were all she needed to travel anywhere. And the songs found the whales for food and brought the whalers home again.

"No woman would kill a whale. Whales give birth to livin' young, they don't lay eggs like fish. They feed their babies with milk from their breasts, like women, and we never killed them. The man who killed the whale never tasted whale meat from the time of his first kill until after he'd retired as a whaler. And neither did his wife, because he had to be purified and linked to the whale and the link was through his wife, by way of the woman's blood and the woman's milk. This was a promise made by Copper Woman, through the magic women, to the whales. No one linked to them will eat them. It is a promise.

"Only certain women could marry whalers and whalers could only marry certain women, and there had to be a bond between them that went farther and deeper than the bond between man and woman, flesh and warmth: it had to be a bond of soul and spirit. If the bond got broken or the trust betrayed, the whales wouldn't come, the people went without and the whaler had to purify himself. If he didn't, or couldn't, the link stayed broken and he was finished as a whaler.

"For a certain time before he went whalin', they wouldn't touch each other like man and woman, like husband and wife, and they prayed certain prayers and ate certain food and stored up their soul energy.

"Then they'd go to the sacred fresh-water pool and they'd sing and dance, and bathe in the water, and clean themselves with hemlock and fir, and slap their skins to move the blood fast in their veins, and they'd pray.

"Then the woman, when she felt her energy was high, would run to the salt chuck as fast as she could and sit in water up to her neck, and she'd watch the sea and pray.

"The man would stay on the beach and pray and direct his soul energy to the woman, to help, and she'd send part of herSelf out to the whales and the link would be made, to him through her, because of the blood and the milk.

"They'd go back to the village and he'd go off after the whales, and the whole time he was gone she'd lie in her bed and stay linked and not eat. And if he got killed, she knew it first, and sometimes she'd die, too. Not always. Sometimes."

Granny's foot stopped wiggling, her leg quit moving, and she looked up at us. "We're nearly there," she smiled, and she hopped down off the fish box, stiffer than a kid but looking like one.

"Do you know all the songs?" Big Bill asked.

"The sickness killed off the songs." Granny shook her head sadly. "So many people died. So many songs and stories and sea routes and histories. I only know a few of them."

Then she grinned and reached for the picnic basket. "But I can always find this place."

STONES

"They brought her here. Copper Woman. The magic women brought her here when they came to make sure she was all right after the flood..."

We left the boat anchored and came ashore in the rubber dinghy, and dragged it up on the sand where it'd be safe. We didn't eat any clams or oysters because it was salmonberry and blackberry time, when the red tide is most liable to bloom, but we had potato salad and crab and smoked salmon and cold beer, and if the Queen of England had been there she'd have said she'd never eaten anything better, and she'd have been as stuffed full and lazy as we were.

But no way would my Granny let us sleep off all that good food and beer. We were all put to work with lard pails and water buckets, picking blackberries, because when my Granny makes jam, you pick until you don't care if you see another berry or bush as long as you live. Granny picked right along with us, and sometimes her mouth was as busy as her gnarled old fingers.

"We had things we had to do," she told Liniculla, Suzy's little girl, "and we hadda do 'em, too. Learnin' to weave baskets and rain capes from cedar bark or from special grass, learnin' how to comb the little white dogs we had so their long fur could be spun and made into warm vests. Lots of things we hadda learn, boys and girls alike. And every day we had to get our bodies ready. So that when the time came to go from bein' a girl to bein' a woman, we'd be ready.

"Swimmin'. We did a lot of swimmin'. Winter and summer. Sometimes we'd get a rope around our waists and get tied to a log and have to swim and swim and swim without ever gettin' anywhere, just swimmin' until we were so tired we ached, but our muscles got strong and our bodies grew straight. Winter or summer, we had to swim. The chuck isn't much warmer in summer than in winter, which doesn't mean it's warm in winter, just that it's still cold and dangerous in summertime. You aren't apt to wind up in trouble out there on a nice sunny day. The dangerous time is when it's stormy and the water sure isn't warm then! So even when it was snowy or frosty, we swam.

"And we'd run. Didn't matter if you ran fast or not, you ran, up and down the beach in your bare feet until your feet were tough and it didn't matter if you stepped on a shell or a barnacle or a sharp stick. Up and down, up and down, and just when we thought we were gettin' good at it they told us we had to learn to run without kickin' any sand.

"You try it sometime. Even walkin', the sand comes up from your feet and blows in the wind. Well, they showed us how to do it. Over and over they showed us how to do it. And we'd try. Just when we thought it was impossible for anybody to do it, one of the sisters would run past, and there'd be no sand comin' up from her feet, and we'd start all over again. My back ached sometimes from tryin' to do that. And then one day, just like that, I could walk without sprayin' sand."

She laughed, looking down at Liniculla, who was staring up at Granny, her soft girl-mouth half open, her dark eyes almost eating Granny's face.

"Then I had to start all over again, learnin' how to run. You had to learn or you weren't a woman. It isn't easy becomin' a woman, it's not somethin' that just happens because you've been standin' around in one place for a long time, or because your body's started doin' certain things. A woman has to know patience, and a woman has to know how to stick it out, and a woman has to know all kinds of things that don't just come to you like a gift. There was always a reason for the things we hadda learn, and sometimes you'd been a woman for a long time before you found out for yourself what the reason was. But if you hadn't learned, you couldn't get married or have children, because you just weren't ready, you didn't know what needed to be known to do it right.

"And the thing of it is," Granny said, sitting down in the shade of a small fir tree. She poured tea from her thermos into her red plastic cup, sipped and nodded satisfaction. She offered the cup to Liniculla, who plopped herself down immediately and smiled, then said her thank-yous properly, in our language. "It wasn't just the girls had to do this hard stuff," Granny went on. "Boys had to do things, too. They were at their own beach, doin' the swimmin' until they ached, same as us. They had to learn to run without kickin' up sand or leavin' big, deep footprints behind 'em. They had to learn the names and uses of all the trees, learn how to fish, learn how to take wood from a tree without choppin' it down, they learned the same stuff we learned, but they didn't learn from the sisters. When a little boy was born, his mother's brothers took over the responsibility for bein' sure he was properly educated. Now let's just say you're old enough, and all trained and ready, and you want to marry this lovely gorgeous boy from, oh, say Queen's Cove. Well, your whole entire family isn't going to move up there with you. No. A family up there who are the same clan as you would formally offer to stand in. There'd be a big ceremony up there and your family would go up for it and they'd accept the offer, and they'd do certain things, and then, you see, your family would, like, adopt the other family. That made the other family, the stand-in family, part of your family. You didn't become part of theirs. That was important. Real important. Then the young men from the stand-in family would promise that they would be full uncles to any boy babies that were born. And the young women would promise they would be full aunties to any girl that got born. Sometimes, not always but sometimes, they even swapped names so your babies would always know they had, say, an Aunt Lin. And then when you brought 'em back down home for visits, there'd be an Aunt Lin for 'em, all over again.

"So, let's see, we've sent you off to Queen's Cove to marry this gorgeous boy, and you've got your stand-in family up there, and you have a baby. A baby boy, say.

"Well, his stand-in uncles would make sure he learned boy things. Of course, his daddy would, too, but he'd have obligations to *his* nephews as well. And when it was time for your son to learn, oh, let's say he has to learn how to catch cod.

Well, his stand-in uncles would take him with them when they went for cod, and they'd show him and let him try it, and if he actually caught one, the celebration when he got back would make him feel real proud and he'd want to catch more so's he could help feed all the people. And if you'd had a girl, her stand-in aunties would be there for her, and so would a stand-in granny and grandpa. Which is like how I'm your granny even though I'm not your momma's blood.

"Because your own granny died, and your granny's mom is gone, and there wasn't any granny left on this earth for you. And anyway I love you madly and crazy-like, and I'd rather have you than a new fluffy kitten." And Granny grabbed Lin in one of her one-armed hugs, then rubbed her smooth old hand back and forth on Lin's cheek. It looks rough when she does that, it looks as if she's being real careless, but her touch is like the flutter of a butterfly's wing. Whenever she does that to a kid the kid starts out laughing, because it's so much like wrestling, but then the laugh just changes in their throat and becomes a sound that's a lot like purring.

We've got one kid living with us now who's a real mess. His mom is one of the ones ran off and got tangled up with all the wrong stuff in the city. She had him when she was only about fourteen years old, and by then she was in deep trouble. He was actually born in the infirmary of a girls' detention place, and he went to a foster home until she got out and satisfied them that she was what they called on her feet. She was in a foster home herself, and going back to school and acting as if she'd learned the lessons, and she kept saying she wanted her baby. So finally, when the kid was about a year, year and a half old, they let her have him. Two months later she skips out of the foster home and she's down in the skids living with a guy old enough to be her grandpa, and they're boozing and partying, and sometimes they might have a sitter but probably not, or if they did have, the sitter might or might not look after the kid. It was crazy.

Then she got picked up and the welfare scooped the kid and put him in a foster home. She could only see him under supervision, but of course she saw him at the foster home so she knows where he is, and one day she goes and scoops him, and on and on, until there he is and he's ten years old and he's been in and out of every kind of situation and he's tough as an old boot.

There's this old white guy, a real head-case, he likes to pick up hookers and then get them so drunk they die. Once they're dead he has sex with them. Or on them. So he meets up with this kid's momma in a chintzy pub and she tells him it's going to be however much money for a trick, and he says how much for the whole entire night and she tells him, and he says let's go, and she goes with him because he pays her right then and there. Well, they go to this hotel, a real scuzzy hole of a one, and he has all this booze and they keep drinking, only he isn't really drinking, and she gets totally drunk and he even gives her some of what they call controlled substance to smoke, and then he starts doing this thing where he'll pour her a full glass of something and hold out a twenty and say give you twenty if you can chug-a-lug it, so she does. So there she is, and she's dead as a post.

He goes down to the desk and he says call an ambulance. His story is he was asleep, he woke up, and she was… The thing of it is you might get away with that once or twice, but the cops charge him with something, reckless endangerment or something. And there's the kid, they've got him in a foster home again, and he runs away and they scoop him and put him in a facility and he's like a savage animal. They try this and they try that and then his poor momma's auntie goes over there and says you're going to make him crazy for all the days of his life the way you're going about it. He's ours, she says, and we couldn't have him sooner because his momma wouldn't agree but we're taking him now. They got nothing else that seems to be working so they go along with it, and she comes back to us with this kid who's like a feral tomcat.

They can't handle him. None of us can handle him. He doesn't just get in fights with other kids, he tries to kill them, uses anything he can get his hands on. Steals, lies, cheats, fights, mouths back at people. Finally he goes that one step too far and his old uncle, who isn't his uncle but was his mom's uncle, he grabs that little sucker and plants him in a boat with another guy and takes him off to one of the islands. It's one we used in the old days. Plenty of water, and a little hut-house with a sort of a stove. The uncle gets off the boat with him. The other guy leaves the two of them with a big whack of groceries, and there they are. Just that kid and this older uncle guy. They're out there two, three months and the uncle treats that kid the way they used to, before schools and stuff. One day the other guy comes over to bring them some groceries and the uncle says, next time you come we're heading back with you.

Be nice if it worked first time, but nothing ever does. They're back in the village and things are definitely better, but not enough for anyone to relax around that head-case kid. They go back to that island twice, and each time the kid comes back a bit better. The last time they went over, the uncle took two other kids, same age. Both of them are thought of as being good boys. Uncle says he's not worried the head-case kid will teach the other boys bad things, he's pretty sure it'll work the other way around. He says the thing the kid needs to learn is how to not expect everyone else to be on the prod against him.

The last time they were back in the village, this kid went to a softball game, and he's yelling at the players and telling them they're lousy and don't know what they're doing, and he's running off at the mouth and being disrespectful, and my Granny just grabs him the way she grabbed Liniculla. No warning, nothing, she just grabs him in what the wrestlers call a headlock. He gets all set to fight, and she gives him that face rub and all that mouth-shit coming out of him stops. Just stops dead, right in the middle of eff-you. And he stands there, stiff as a post while she gives him the butterfly rub. Then she lets go of the headlock and that kid stood there as if he'd been frozen in place, kind of half bent forward and a bit sideways, and you could *see* the tears pouring from his eyes. My Granny said something to him that nobody else could hear and he said, clear as a bell, yes, ma'am, and she walked off with him. Just walked off with him. Ball game continues, nobody follows. I started to, but Big Bill clamped onto my arm and said butt out. So I did.

When the ball game is finished and the daylight is fading, I go home and there's my Granny, sitting on the sofa in front of the TV, with this brat of a kid lying with his head in her lap, and he's asleep. His eyes are all swelled up from tears and his face is still blotchy from crying, and he's asleep altogether. I said I'd put him to bed and my Granny just shook her head and didn't speak to me, so I knew it was butt-out time again and I did, all the way out, and I went over to Suzy's place for the night. Which I often do, anyway.

I went back over first thing in the morning and there was my Granny, still sitting on that sofa, and she was asleep and that wild boy was asleep too, with his head in her lap. I didn't know if I should stay or go, so I stayed and started breakfast. They woke up and they washed up, then they ate and then that kid, he gave my Granny a little bit of a hug. Not much, but more than he'd volunteered to anyone else, and then he left and went to the older uncle and said, please can we go to the island? That's when the uncle rounded up those other two and took them along. I tried to talk to my Granny about it but she said I didn't have to know, and furthermore I wasn't ready to know, so I guess about all I can do is wait. I don't know if that boy, that poor crazy boy, is going to get healed or if he'll slit the other three's throats some night. I guess it could go either way.

"So when I got to where I could finally run in the sand," Granny continued, "and not spray it all over the beach, I had to learn to do it backwards. You try that sometime." She got to her feet and moved back to a berry bush, with Lin as good as glued to her. "You think you got good balance because you can walk on top of a fence and not fall off? You try runnin' backwards, see how much balance you got.

"And runnin' in water. First only to your ankles, so it dragged at your feet, and then deeper and deeper until you're in water halfway up your thighs, runnin' as fast as you can, and all that water has to be pushed out of the way. Ki-Ki can do it, that's why she's got such nice legs.

"Of course," and she shot me a look with her sideways eyes, "it makes your bum stick out a bit, like a half a pumpkin on a plank, but that looks nice, too," and she laughed again and went to dump her lard pail full of berries into the bigger water pail.

"When you'd learned everythin' you had to learn, and the Time was right, and you'd had your first bleedin' time and been to the waitin' house, there was a big party. You were a woman. Everyone knew you were a woman. And people would come from other places, uncles and aunts and cousins and friends, and there'd be singin' and dancin' and lots of food. Then they'd take you in a special dugout, all decorated up with waterbird down, the finest feathers off the breast of the bird, and you'd have on all your best clothes and all your crests, and you'd stand up there so proud and happy. They'd chant a special chant, and the old woman would lead 'em, and they'd take you a certain distance. When the chant ended, the old woman would sing a special prayer and take off all your clothes, and you'd dive into the water, and the dugout would go home. And you'd be out there in the water all by yourself, and you had to swim back to the village.

"The people would watch for you and light fires on the beach, and when they finally saw you they'd start to sing a victory song about how a girl went for a swim and a woman came home, and you'd make it to the beach and your legs would feel like they were made of rocks or somethin'. You'd try to stand up and you'd shake all over, just plain wore out. And then the old woman, she'd come up and put her cape over you and you'd feel just fine. And after that, you were a woman, and if you wanted to marry up with someone, you could, and if you wanted to have children, you could, because you'd be able to take care of them the proper way.

"Every month, when the moontime came for you, you'd go to the waitin' house and have a four-day holiday, or a party. Most of the women had their moontime at about the same time of the month, and you'd sit on a special moss paddin' and give the blood of your body back to the Earth Mother, and you'd play games and talk, and if you were havin' cramps there was a special tea you could drink and they'd go away, and the other sisters would rub your back. We'd play Frog if the cramps were a bother. You scrunch down, like this." Granny dropped to the ground to demonstrate. "Tuck your knees up under your belly, and put your head down with your forehead on the ground, and then curl your back like a cat, like this, and breathe in deep, and then straighten your back. Looks funny, but it works. It's good when you first start havin' your baby, too, makes everythin' shift into the right place."

Liniculla dropped to the ground beside Granny and tried the position, and Suzy and I watched, looking at each other with quick looks, both of us blinking to keep from getting all watery-eyed as the girl who was years away from starting her menstrual cycle, and the woman who had finished hers years before, practised the cramp-stopping position.

"That's right." Granny got up, a bit stiffly. "Now you don't have to ever worry about gettin' bad cramps or havin' to take pills or anythin'. Just do the Frog game, and you'll be fine."

All this time Pete had been finding big clumps of berries a few yards farther on from where we were, and he'd call out and we'd move toward them. Even talking to Liniculla, Granny would watch Pete, and from time to time she'd grin a bit to herself. But she was deep in her talk with Liniculla and didn't speak to Pete, although we all knew Pete was listening to what Granny was saying. Finally Pete turned, and smiled, and Granny took an overripe berry and squished it against his nose.

"Some people," she teased him, "are so smart and so fast they're gonna meet themselves comin' back again. Come on then," and she took his hand and headed toward the circle of stones. We all put our buckets and pails down and moved fast to catch up with her.

"This one," she pointed, "was bigger before. Somethin' bust off the top of it, see, it's lyin' off to one side a bit. Don't know what it was broke it off. But I know it used to sit on top, all one piece. The sun ought to set right through that crack." She pointed again. "And if it does, the moon'll come up between them two rocks and move over there before the sun starts to come up over that one."

She knew from the looks on our faces we hadn't understood anything but the words, so she sighed, and sat down on the grass and started to explain, as patient as if she was talking to a pack of two-year-olds.

"The circle isn't complete any more, and nobody knows where the missin' rock went. It was tall and thin and had magic marks on it, to measure with, and it didn't fall over or get dragged away. One time it was here, the next time it wasn't, just a bare patch on the ground where it used to be and no sign of it anywhere. No drag marks, no broken chips or rubble, just... gone.

"The family that knew the full story of the measurin' rocks got the choke-throat sickness, the diphtheria, and what we know now is nothin' to what we used to know. We could measure anythin'. Days, months, years, distance, anythin'."

Pete lay back, staring up at the blue sky, his funny-coloured eyes missing nothing of the cloud formations, his bleached hair blowing in the breeze. He just lay back, waiting for Granny to continue, and when she started talking in our own language he understood what she meant. He didn't understand all the words, but he understood what the words were telling him. Granny's eyes got that faraway other-world look that meant she was seeing things the rest of us couldn't see, and Liniculla stared at her as if watching Granny's face was like watching a movie screen on which she could see the hidden things, too.

"They brought her here. Copper Woman. The magic women brought her here when they came to make sure she was all right after the flood. She went out in her dugout to meet them and they lifted her, dugout and all, and brought her to this place.

"There are other places with other stones in other patterns, but they all do the same thing, they measure and mark. And the big one, the main one, isn't on this coast.

"When they first got here, there were no rocks. Just sea and beach and a big empty field with grass and flowers. In the sand on the beach they drew a big circle and told her the secrets about it, and about how it's the link to the real home, and when she was able to understand, they taught her how to do what they could do, lift up off the ground like dust in the wind, and when she could lift herself and float where she wanted, they showed her how to leave her meat and bones in her sack of skin and just send her Self someplace else.

"When she could do that, they told her how some bodies in the sky never change, and others do. And when she understood all that, and could find the ones that never, not ever, change, they did their magic and they cut the rocks from the mountain and shaped them the way they wanted them, and then, the same way they moved themselves, they moved the stones and set them in place and marked them, and set the rock that's missin' now in its place and put magic marks on it, and taught her about measurin' and how to use the measures and the rocks to figure out distance and time.

"And with the rocks and the stars and the measurements, and Klin Otto, we always knew where we were and how much was ours." The faraway look began to fade, and Granny focussed on Pete, then smiled at him and held out her hand. He reached over and took her hand in his and they sat there, just holding hands and looking at each other. "We were able to measure and mark off which section of the river was where this family had first-fishing rights, and which section was where another family did. We could measure the beach and say who had the inherited right to dig clams or such. And the ones who had the inherited right, they got first dibs. They might invite someone else to go with them, but that didn't mean that other person could just keep going there, and it didn't mean they could go without the ones with the inherited right. There's some say we didn't have any concept of personal ownership. That's just silly. We did. We had some very clear and very strict rules of ownership. We just didn't interpret 'own' the same way. Like the way it is now, a person can 'own' something and neglect it or even trash it all to hell and gone and because he 'owns' it, nobody can argue about it.

"But just because you had inherited ownership didn't give you the right to mess up a place. And if you didn't take care of it, you could lose it. That didn't happen much, because if one person who was supposed to be in charge of a place didn't bother, some other family members would take up the slack. So if you had inherited ownership of a section of the river, say, you were expected and obligated to keep it in really good condition. You went there at change-of-season, which is four times a year, and you cleaned up any fallen branches or logs or such, and you made sure your spawning banks were in good shape. Sometimes you'd go there when the water was low and there would be lots of little fish stranded in pools. Left alone, they'd die in the warm water. The sun would do what it always does, the water in the pools would get shallower and warmer until there was no oxygen in it for the fish. But if it was your section of the river, you'd go and you could make, like, channels from one pool to another and scoop out the baby fish or chase 'em down the channel you'd made until you had 'em back in the river, in the deeper, cool water. One time, on our section of the river, we took waterproof baskets and filled 'em halfways full of water, then we scooped out baby fish that were stranded, worked at it for three days, got them moved into the river again, and we counted more than fifteen hundred of 'em.

That's a good feeling. Four years later they come back to spawn and you can sit on the riverbank and watch 'em and think, that's because of *me*.

"And the thing was, you inherited ownership of the stretch of riverbank and you inherited the obligations and responsibilities, and you could set your nets from the bank out into the river, but other people could use the middle of the river, they didn't just set nets. They'd come and they'd use hook and line.

"And fish come in more than one wave. They don't all swarm up the creek at the same time. First bunch comes in and you do not catch any of 'em. You watch 'em, you even help 'em, and only when they've spawned, and you know the gravel banks are well nested and the second bunch are startin' to head on up, do you start settin' nets. Sometimes we'd dip-net, and that was fun. You'd be on a high bank, say, or a bluff or a cliff over a rough part, sometimes you had to have a rope tied around your waist so's you could lean way way out and dip into the water with your long-handled net. And when you caught a fish, or a bunch of fish, you didn't just kill 'em, you milked 'em first. Male or female you milked 'em into a waterproof basket, and when you were just about ready to go home you'd find a sandbar or a gravel bank and you'd do what the fish did, you'd make like a little trough or nest or like that, and then carefully, carefully you'd empty your basket of fertilized eggs into it and gently, gently you'd cover the eggs with fine gravel. They wouldn't all hatch, but some would. Plenty would. And then four years later they'd all come back again, and *all* the people would have a chance to catch 'em, because of you and what you'd done. So even if you had ownership, you didn't hog anythin' away from everyone else. Havin' ownership just meant you had responsibility. You'd been chosen, you see, your whole family had been chosen, to look after and take care of something. And that gave you first dibs but it didn't mean you could be piggy."

CLOWNS

"But mostly the clowns were very serious about what they did. And the most famous clown was a woman who wasn't even one of us..."

It was coming on Hallowe'en and the whole village was getting itself involved. The people had stacked driftwood in a hollow square on the beach until it was too tall for a man standing on another man's shoulders to add anything more, and then they all set about filling up the hollow centre with burnable junk, garbage, old newspapers, whatever was lying around that would burn. We kind of clean up the village every year this way. Just down the beach some, we built a second square and filled it, too, but that wasn't for Hallowe'en. It was for something else, and you'll find out about that later.

Every window had a scary black cat or a big orange pumpkin Scotch-taped to it, and the closer it got to being the end of the month, the more frantic the kids got in their search for costumes. Liniculla was driving us all crazy. First it was a pirate, but she decided her legs would get cold in the raggedy-bottom cut-off pants. Then it was a princess, but she changed her mind about that, too; she didn't think a princess would be wearing a net curtain as a veil. I was just about ready to tell her to go as a sack of spuds, and I had the sack to dump her into, too, when Granny put in her two bits worth.

"A clown," she suggested.

"Everybody goes as a clown!" Liniculla shot that idea down in a rush. "Going as a clown means you couldn't think of a real costume to wear."

"Not a circus clown," Granny corrected quietly. When Lin gets hyper and her voice rises and she starts to sound like someone who needs a quick smack on the seat of learning, Granny's voice gets softer and softer, until she's almost whispering. Somehow that calms Lin down quicker than anything. Maybe because she has to stop yelling so she can hear Granny speak. "One of our clowns," Granny went on. "Like in the days before the invaders came."

"We didn't have clowns, did we?" Liniculla asked, already making herself comfortable at Granny's feet, waiting eagerly for another story.

"We had clowns," Granny smiled, reaching for the brush for Liniculla's long hair. "Not clowns like you see now, with round red noses and baggy costumes. Our clowns wore all different kinds of stuff. Anythin' they felt like, they wore. And they didn't just come out once in a while to act silly and make people laugh. Our clowns were with us all the time, as important to the village as the chief, or the shaman, or the dancers, or the poets.

"A clown was like a newspaper, or a magazine, or one of those people who write an article to tell you if a book or a movie is worth botherin' with. They made comment on everythin', every day, all the time. If a clown thought that what the tribal council was gettin' ready to do was foolish, why the clown would just show up at the council and imitate every move every one of the leaders made. Only the clown would imitate it in such a way that every little wart on that person would show, every hole in their idea would suddenly look real big.

"It was like if you were real vain about your clothes, all of a sudden, the clown would be there, walkin' right behind you, all decked out in the most godawful mess of stuff, but all of it lookin' somehow like what you were wearin'. Maybe you had a necklace you always wore and showed off, well, the clown would have bits of bark and twigs, and feathers and dog shit, and old broken clam shells, and just about anythin' else you can think of, and it'd all be made up in a necklace like yours. And if you walked a certain way because you were vain, the clown would walk the way you did. Where you had on your best clothes, the clown would be in rags and tatters and old bits of fern and you name it, and the clown's hair would look like a bird's nest, all mud and sticks and crap. And everywhere you went, the clown would go. Everythin' you did, the clown did. And nobody would ever dare blow up at the clown! If you did that, well, you were totally shamed. A clown didn't do what a clown did to hurt you or make fun of you or be mean, it was to show you what you looked like to other people, let you see for yourself just how foolish it is to get yourself all tied in knots over some clothes and stuff instead of what counts, like bein' nice to people, and bein' lovin', and tryin' to fit in with the people you live with.

"Or if you thought every word you spoke was gospel, the

clown would just stroll along behind you babblin' away like a simple-mind or a baby. Every up and down of your voice, the clown's voice would go up and down, too, until you finally heard what an ass you were bein'. Or maybe you had a bad temper and yelled a lot and got mad real easy, you hadn't learned any self control. Well, the clown would just have fits. Every time you turned around there'd be the clown bashin' away with a stick on the sand or kickin' like a fool at a big rock, or yellin' insults back at the gulls, and just generally lookin' real stupid.

"We needed our clowns, and we used 'em to help us all learn the best ways to get along with each other. Bein' an individual is real good, but sometimes we're so busy bein' individuals we forget we gotta live with a lot of other people who all got the right to be individuals too, and the clowns could show us if we were gettin' a bit pushy, or startin' to take ourselves too seriously. Wasn't nothin' sacred to a clown. Sometimes a clown would find another clown taggin' along behind, imitatin', and then the first one knew that maybe somethin' was gettin' out of hand, and maybe the clown was bein' mean or usin' her position as a clown to push people around and sharpen her own axe for her own reasons.

"But mostly the clowns were very serious about what they did. And the most famous clown was a woman who wasn't even one of us. She lived on the other side of the island with the Salish people. Or maybe it was the Cowichan, I guess I'm not too clear about that. Must be gettin' old. Anyway, this woman had been a clown all her life. Ever since she was a girl she'd been able to imitate people, how they walked, how they talked, so she was trained to do it properly for the right reasons, not just to get attention.

"The Christian people were dividin' up the island. This bunch got this part and another bunch got another part, and they built their churches and set about gettin' us into them. There's people say that it used to be we had the land and the white man had the Bible, now all we've got is the Bible and the white man's got the land. When you look at it, that's not far from wrong—except lots of us don't even got the Bible. Anyway, they'd built this stone church on a hill, with a cross on top of it pointin' up at the sky, and the preacher, he was gettin' people to come to church by givin' out little pictures and mirrors and such, things we didn't have. Might not seem like much now, a mirror, but they were as rare as diamonds, and it's bein' rare makes a thing worth a lot. Like roses are worth more than dandelions because there aren't so many of them, but they're both flowers.

"So the people started goin' to this church, and pretty soon it was the same old story. They started gettin' told what to do, and what to wear, and how to live, and this particular preacher, he was big on what they ought to wear. He didn't want the men wearin' kilts, he wanted 'em in pants, and he didn't want the women in anythin' but long dresses that covered 'em completely. And he kept tellin' everyone to learn to live like the white man, dress like the white man.

"Well, one Sunday didn't the clown show up. She was wearin' a big black hat, just like a white man, and a black jacket just like a white man, and old rundown shoes some white man had thrown away. And nothin' else."

Liniculla giggled and her eyes sparkled, and Granny just kept brushing that long hair and telling her story.

"Well, the white preacher, he just about had a fit! Here's this woman more naked than not, walkin' into his church, and what's worse, the people in the church are all lookin' at her real respectful, not mockin' her or laughin' or coverin' their eyes so they wouldn't see her nakedness. And she moved to the very front and sat there and waited for the church service to start.

"Well, that preacher, he ranted and raved about nakedness, and naked women, and sin, and havin' respect for God, and then he came down from that pulpit and he grabbed ahold of that clown to throw her out on her bum.

"The people just about ripped him apart. You don't put violent hands on a clown! But the clown, she stopped them from hurtin' him, and then she went up to the front where he'd been, and she spoke to the people in their own language. She said we were all brothers and sisters because we all had Copper Woman as first mother, and were all descended from the four couples who left after the flood. And she said different people had different ways of doin' things, and that didn't mean any one way was Right or any other way was Wrong, it just meant all ways were different. And she said we ought to think how we'd feel if we were far from home, to put ourselves in the white man's place, how would we feel if there were only a few brown faces and lots of white ones, because maybe the preacher felt that way about bein' almost alone with us. And she said that just because he'd done a forbidden thing and got violent with a clown didn't mean that we ought to get just as mixed up and do a forbidden thing like get violent with a religious man. And she said we all had to find our own way in the world, we all had to find what was true, and what meant somethin'. She said there was more than one kind of mirror. There was the white man's mirror that you got if you went to church, but there was the mirror in the eyes of the people you loved, and what it meant to them when you listened to someone who was so mixed up they'd do forbidden things.

"And then she walked out of the church and all the people got up and walked out behind her and left the preacher alone. Each one, as they walked past him, they put the stuff he had given them on the pew beside him until there was a little pile of mirrors and beads and other stuff as well. And that church is still there today and it's still empty."

"Tell me more," Liniculla begged.

"Not without a cuppa for my windpipe, I won't," Granny teased, and Liniculla ran to put the kettle on. She rinsed out the teapot and warmed it up, measured the tea carefully, then got cups and saucers, sugar and milk, and had everything all ready by the time the water was bubbling. Granny sat watching her, smiling to herself, and it made me remember being ten myself and wanting to help, and how she always let me, even if it made more work for her. And after she'd had a cup of tea and was sipping a second, Granny started rocking slowly, and soon she was into a second clown story.

"The people were goin' down to Victoria a lot and tradin' with Hudson Bay for things they couldn't get anywhere else. They'd kill seal and otter, more than ever before so they'd be able to trade the skins, and even though everyone knew it couldn't last, even though everyone knew the animals wouldn't be able to survive, nobody seemed willin' to be the first not to do it. It was like they figured it was gonna happen anyway, they might as well get some of it for themselves. And not all of the stuff they traded for was worth anythin'. You make a long trip with a big bundle of furs, and you don't feel like bringin' it all home just because the Hudson Bay man doesn't want to trade for somethin' you want. More and more the company was just handin' out junk, and private traders were steppin' in with a few blue beads and lot of rum, and it was all a real mess.

"And this same clown woman, she took herself down to Victoria and she set up shop right next to Hudson Bay. Hudson Bay would give beads, so she had bits of busted shell. They'd give molasses, so she had wild honey. They'd give rum, so she had some old swamp water. And she sat there. That's all she did, was just sit there. And the people goin' to Hudson Bay saw her, and saw the stuff she had to trade, and they knew what she was tellin' 'em. Some of 'em went inside and traded anyway, but some turned around and went back home, and some even went over and traded with her, and she treated them all real serious, took their furs and gave 'em bits of shell and stuff, and they wore it same as they'd'a wore the beads.

"After a while the Hudson Bay man came out to see why hardly anybody had come to trade and he saw her sittin' there and he just about blew up, took himself off to the Governor and complained about the clown woman. The Governor, he took himself outside and had a look and then told the Hudson Bay man a thing or two, and from then on we got good tradin' stuff.

"The clown woman, she went home, and she thought about

what had happened, and she decided that maybe the Governor wasn't such an ass after all. He knew what she was sayin', all right. She decided maybe she could get him to listen about the rum trade. The Americans were sendin' lots of ships up here, and they wouldn't trade nothin' but rum for furs. First they'd just put a small barrel of rum on the beach, free gratis, and then when the men were all into the rum, why, the Americans would come and trade, and the result of that was pretty awful.

"The clown woman, she set off for Victoria again, and all the people knew she was gonna see the Governor and stop the rum trade. She didn't show up in Victoria, so the people went lookin' for her. Found her dead alongside her dugout, she'd been shot in the head.

"Hadda be a white man done it. We would never do violence to a clown."

Liniculla stared at Granny for the longest time, and even before she opened her mouth we knew that there'd be one little clown on Hallowe'en, all decked out in shells, and bark, and feathers, and bits of stuff, trickin' an' treatin' all over the village, giving us all a chance to see things as they could be.

SONG OF BEAR

"There was a young woman who obeyed all the laws of cleanliness, and never went to the hills durin' her period, and did all the things we're supposed to do, but got loved by a bear anyway..."

It was the time of Suzy's menstrual period. It felt good to be around a woman during her sacred time, good to be able to smell the special body perfume, to share in the specialness of it, expecting my own period to start any day, wondering, as it seemed I always did, how it was that the women of the village mostly all had their periods at around the same time. Finally, since I had never been able to figure it out for myself, I asked my Granny. She looked at me as if she couldn't believe anybody could be so simple, and shook her head gently.

"The light, Ki-Ki," she sighed. "It's because of the light. Used to be, before electricity and strong light made it possible for people to stay up half the night, that we all got up with the sun and went to bed with the sun, and because we all got the same amounts of light and dark, our body time was all the same, and we'd all come full at the same time."

"I don't understand," I admitted, feeling more than a bit dumb.

"Well, I don't either," she snapped. "I don't know if it's somethin' in our eyes, or our heads, or our bellies, or what. I only know that it's got somethin' to do with the light, and since everybody around here goes to bed at about the same time, and gets up at about the same time...do you understand the how and why of the geese going south? Then why do you have to understand this?"

She puttered around the kitchen for a few minutes, sucking her lip, making tsk-tsk noises with her tongue, shooting sideways looks at me, and then she smiled and sat down at the table with me, and took my hand.

"Used to be women weren't allowed to go up the mountain durin' their time. Because of the bears. Bears got big sharp noses, and they'd smell the blood of womantime, and think it was a female bear, and try to mate. Prob'ly didn't intend any harm, but bein' hugged by a big male bear is a good way to wind up in bad shape. So the waitin' house was always protected from the bears, and women stayed out of the mountains.

"There was a young woman—" she whispered the name to me, and nodded, but did not give permission for me to repeat it—not then and not later "—who obeyed all the laws of cleanliness, and never went to the hills durin' her period, and did all the things we're supposed to do, but got loved by a bear anyway. What it was, the bear saw her, and just fell in love. Just as soft, and sappy, and foolish as anybody is when love lightnin' hits her. The bear figured the young woman would be afraid, so it hid in the bushes and never tried to touch her or speak to her, it just watched. Watched with its little round eyes, and shook with love. Watched the young woman fishin' and watched her gatherin' berries. Watched her walkin', and watched her laughin' for days. Shakin' with love and feelin' there would never be any hope for this love.

"Well, one day the young woman came back from gatherin' food and she stopped at the fresh-water pool and took a bath. Stripped off all her clothes, walked slowly to the pool, and swam around a bit. Stood in water halfway up her legs and bent over to wash her face. Lay back in the water and washed her hair. Stood up with her hair drippin' wet down her back, and rubbed her body with soft sand, and twisted this way, and twisted that way and then turned and looked right at the bush where the bear was hidin'.

"'I know you're in there,' the young woman laughed. 'I know you've been following me. Watching me. Scaring fish my way so I could catch them. You come out from that bush and let me see you.'

"And the bear just about swallowed its tongue, but it stood up, sunlight glitterin' on its black fur, and it walked toward the fresh-water pool, just as scared as anybody is when the one you love takes notice of you for the first time.

"'Come into the water,' the young woman invited, and the bear walked into the water, and they swam together, and they splashed each other, and the girl fastened her fingers in the bear's thick fur and the bear swam, pullin' the young woman easily.

"'I love you,' the bear managed, even though its voice was caught in its throat.

"'Why did you hide?' the young woman asked.

"'How could anybody as beautiful as you love a bear?' and a tear trickled from the poor bear's eye.

"Well, the young woman took the bear's head in her lap, and stroked its fur and kissed its nose, and said 'But you're beautiful. Strong, and gentle, and beautiful, and I do love you.'

"'I'm a female bear,' the bear said.

"The young woman sat for a long long time, and then she laughed and said, 'If I can love a creature that looks as different from me as you do, why should I care if you are a male bear or a female bear? I love you, bear. I wouldn't not love you if you were skinny, or if you were fat, or if you were shorter, or if you were taller, because it's the love in you that I love, and the beauty in you that I love. Anyway,' the young woman laughed, 'meat and bones don't matter, it's what's inside them, the love spirit.'

"And she stood up and the bear stood up and the young woman put on her dress, and took the bear's paw and walked off with her, up the mountain to the cave where the bear lived, and they went inside and they loved each other. In the cold winter they slept together and the bear's thick fur kept them both warm, and in the springtime they came from the cave together and danced, and fished, and were happy. And the bear wrote a song for the young woman and sang to her, and the young woman was happy. And if people talked about it, they talked about the wonder of a woman and a bear livin' together and bein' happy, because the arrangement of meat and bones doesn't mean anythin'."

And then my Granny sang the song of bear for me and said I could write it down and share it. Anybody who can find

music for this song, and sing it, or dance to it, is a sister of the
bears and can ask to be admitted to the Bear Clan. And when
you go in the mountains, whether it is your menstrual time or
not, you wear a bell, so the bears will hear you and know you
are their friend.

>The spirit of beauty
>has come with me.
>The spirit of beauty
>has left her friends and family
>to come with me.
>Should her family come
>and take her from me
>I would die.
>
>The spirit of beauty
>walks with me.
>I will gather berries for her
>and tubers and roots from the hills.
>I will bend myself to please her,
>will dance for her, keep her warm.
>I wrote this song for her
>I sing it now for her
>
>The spirit of beauty
>has come with me.

QUEEN MOTHER

"When I was young they told me if a generation of people got pushed to killin' other people, it took four generations of peace to get people's heads fixed afterward. And we hadn't had them four generations…"

Granny was knitting a sweater for Liniculla, her big white plastic needles clicking together steadily, the thick natural wool smelling faintly oily in the warm kitchen, the Eagle-Flies-High pattern unfolding on the back of the sweater, black against the unbleached tan-grey of the main wool. Every so often she'd hold both needles in her left hand and, with her right, reach for her cup of wild rosehip tea and take a sip. Granny had sneezed getting out of bed that morning and had been flooding herself with rosehip tea ever since to ward off the cold she was convinced was trying to catch her. I told her she might save herself the cold at the expense of her kidneys, but she just muttered insults in our language about cold pills and tiny time-release and kept on guzzling her herbs.

Suzy and Liniculla had come over after lunch and Suzy tried to check Granny out, make sure she was still strong as a deer, but Granny just shook her off and said she didn't need to be fussed over, she just needed lots of rosehip tea. We decided then and there to leave her alone before she got herself in a bad mood and told us all to leave the house for a few days.

"My grandmother was the Queen Mother," she said suddenly and flatly, replacing her cup and picking up her knitting again. "Her son was the king. She wasn't Queen Mother because he was the king, like in England. He was king only because she was Queen Mother. His son wouldn't inherit to be king. The Queen Mother's oldest girl, my mother, would become Queen Mother and *her* son—my brother—would have been king. I would have been Queen Mother after my mother because I was the oldest girl, and my son would have been king. Your mother, Ki-Ki, would have been Queen Mother, and if you'd had a brother, he'd have been king. Then you'd have been Queen Mother and your son would have been king.

"Only it all got buggered," she amended calmly, flashing a funny twisted smile at Suzy and me. "Got real buggered because the ships came back and instead of chasin' them away because of what had happened before, the people hoped this time it would be different.

"Maquinna, he was maybe thirty when they came back. First the Spaniards, then the English hot on their tails, and already we knew about the missions in California and explorin' ships sailin' all over everywhere lookin' for places to claim. Maquinna figured it was like swimmin' upstream against a flood. Salmon do it to spawn, but then they all die, so he talked about makin' the best of things and bendin' like a willow when the storms blow and, in spite of everythin', I expect he was right. When it's time for a thing to change, it's Time for a thing to change, and it changes.

"Things weren't all fine and easy any more, anyway. When people get pushed to the point where killin' seems the only way, somethin' happens to them. They get jerked around inside somehow, and it takes a long time to get right again. When I was young they told me if a generation of people got pushed to killin' other people, it took four generations of peace to get people's heads fixed afterward. And we hadn't had them four generations.

"We came back from killin' off the Keestadores and burnin' a third of the island flat, and we were all more'n a bit haywire. Seems like power does what booze does, just makes a person thirsty for more. The men had filled themselves with power, bashin' in heads and spillin' blood, and some of the women were the same. Families started lookin' on power as somethin' to have. Somethin' they needed. Power itself doesn't have to be bad, it's how you use it, I guess. Some of them still had guns they'd taken from Keestadores, and not all of the gunpowder got blown up in the mine.

"First it was little stuff, then it got worse. The Manhousats and Ahousats kept arguin' over fishin' rights and land measure. The family that knew the full story of the measurin' rocks and coulda settled the mess were missin' some of their people, so neither of the bunches arguin' would believe what they got told, and they said the story was incomplete. The next thing you know, they were at it for sure. Doesn't matter who started it or why, some say it was the Manhousats, some say it was the Ahousats, the end of it was the Ahousats wiped out most all of the Manhousats and moved to their island and they're still there.

"Raidin' parties went around the island and over to the mainland and up the big river to raid the interior people and bring home slaves and women. It was all pretty haywire altogether, and the women they stole and brought down, they hadn't been brought up the same way, and that caused some trouble and hard feelin', too.

"Slaves had always been part of things, but they'd never been abused before, no more'n a city person would buy an expensive horse and then starve it. A person didn't have slaves to do work, a person had 'em to show there was food enough to feed 'em. But that got buggered, too.

"There's people talk like it was pure paradise here before Cook came, but it wasn't. Prob'ly never had been. Sure not if you were a slave. The carvers who made the dugouts did the whole job while the tree was still standin', they cut out the dugout until it was just the top bit and bottom bit holdin' it to the tree. And they believed that the first thing the dugout touched, it would marry, so if it married the earth, it wouldn't float, and would go up on rocks tryin' to get back to what it married. So they'd lower it by pulleys and levers and such and roll it on wooden rollers all the way to the water. If it didn't ride right, or sunk when it touched water, the carver'd be so shamed he might kill himself. But after a while, just to show he was powerful and rich enough to afford it, a man would lay down slaves instead of alder poles, and run the big dugouts over them to the water, killin' and cripplin' them, and when the holy people said it was wrong, well, nobody listened.

"Then the dugouts came sayin' Cook was lost in the fog,

and they went out and steered him in to a safe place and gave him and his starvin' sailors food, and for their trouble, they got sick. The Queen Mother's son, he was sick for some months, then he seemed to get better, but a year or two later he started coughin' blood and him and his wife and kids all died. Lots of people died."

She measured the sweater against Liniculla's back, and Suzy poured her more rosehip tea. I put a stick of wood on the fire, but it was more to listen to it crackle than to heat the kitchen.

"That meant the next oldest boy was king and he did fine at that job. Had sense enough to ask for help if he needed it, which is more than can be said for some.

"When the Queen Mother died, her oldest girl, my mother, became Queen Mother, only she never did have a son live long enough to become king, so her brother, my uncle, stood in as best he could. Things were real bad. People dyin' all over everywhere. One day there was no smoke at all from the village at Hecate, so the people from Kyuquot sent over a dugout to check, and they found the whole village dead. Every last one of 'em, lyin' in their own mess and covered with sores. The Kyuquots stayed to try to burn the dead, do things properly, and before they'd finished, they were sick too. They headed home and took the sickness with them, and soon Kyuquot was under a thick smoke from the crematin' fires. People were burnin' up with fever so bad they'd run to the sea to cool off and the shock of the cold water on their burnin' bodies would stop their hearts, and they'd fall dead.

"My uncle did the best he could but the people were goin' crazy from havin' everyone they knew drop dead like that. My mother's sons all died young and by the time I was twelve my mother and my uncles were all dead, too.

"I was twelve and just finishin' my puberty trainin' and already I was Queen Mother. I had five uncles and two aunts and they were all married with big families, and my mother had four sons and five daughters but there I was gettin' ready for my big swim, and there was just me and my younger sister left. My sister, she had some spot scars on her face, but I only had some on my back and on one leg.

"They took me out in the dugout, like they'd always done, and I stood in the seabird down, in all my best clothes and things, and they sang and they chanted, but they cried, too. The old woman, she stood near me, and she cried the whole way out, and it felt weird. I felt so proud and so happy that I'd finished my woman trainin', and I felt so sad and scared because I knew, even if nobody else did, that I wasn't ready to be no Queen Mother.

"There wasn't nothin' else to do, though. I stripped off my stuff and I dove in the water and I started to swim back, chantin' the song in my head and strokin' in time to the music. I just did what I'd been trained to do, even though I knew there'd be no mother and father waitin', proud and happy, and no aunts or grandmother. I cried, too. Salt tears and salt water, and the cold cuttin' into me, and once I almost just gave up and let the sea have me, but I knew my sister would have even more trouble than me, so I kept goin'. She hadn't been trained to be Queen Mother, and it wouldn't have been fair to her. Or to the others who had already lost so much, practically their whole world. And then I stepped out on the beach, and I fell down, and Old Woman was cryin' and so was I, and then she put her cape around me and I just knew that's it, it's okay, nothin' else will be this bad. This is as worse as it can get and you made it through and it won't ever be this bad again.

"They had mission schools by then. Not government residential schools like came later, but church schools, and they started takin' the orphans and lookin' after them, even though the ones who'd survived were more than willin' to have those kids. They came for my sister'n'me, but I ran off and hid and the people said I'd died. They believed that, since so many others had died already. And they only took my sister.

"I was supposed to be Queen Mother and I almost needed babysittin' myself. Stuff I shoulda learned had died when the memorizers choked on diphtheria or died from whoopin' cough or rottin' sickness. The old women taught me what they knew, and Old Woman, she taught what she knew, and I stayed clear of the mission schools, so it wasn't too bad. My sister, she was there until she turned fifteen. Then she'd learned all they had to teach, and she wanted to come home. But they said no, she hadda have someone to look after her. Never figured she could look after her own self. That's how good the stuff was that they made her learn. So she had to stay two more years, workin' for them until she could arrange with a young man who wanted to go home, to marry her, and so they let 'em both come home. She had a little girl the next year and a boy two years later but she died havin' him, so there was just me. I had plenty of room in my place for those kids and I was lookin' after them, because I was their auntie and that's what aunties do, but the mission people came with the constables and took them and their dad. He had been mission-trained and it never even entered his head to say no, leave 'em where they are.

"I hadn't really thought much about gettin' married, but I didn't feel that it was what I wanted, and in the old days that might have been allowed, what with my sister havin' a boy to be king. But things had changed, and the boy wasn't with us, and it wasn't the old days. And finally, after listenin' a lot to the others, well, I figured I'd better get married and have some kids while there was still someone alive to be the father, and I got married. Twice. First husband, he gave me two boys, then he went down in his fish boat and we never found his body. My oldest son by him woulda been king, but they took him to residential school and he got the TB, so they took him to hospital in Nanaimo, but he died there. I got married a second time just before he died, to your grandpa. We had a boy, then your momma. The second boy from my first husband came back from residential school real mesatchie, and he went off to be a logger and got to drinkin' and took his car off the road and that was that.

"Your momma was six and I had another little boy, and they took your momma off to residential school, and then the baby, he got sick and they said he should go to Nanaimo, too. So I talked to your grandpa and I told him I was tired of cryin' over kids that got took away from me and he agreed with me. From then on I drank the bug-weed tea and made sure I knew where the moon was all the time.

"Then your grandpa, he died. Big strong man, always laughin, always lovin'. He caught the measles from some kids and he died. Your momma ran away from residential school and haywired around Vancouver for a couple of years, and then, when she got out of jail, she came home and married up with your daddy. I never had much use for him or his family, myself, but your momma figured his summer socks were perfumed and he was real good to her. He'd brush her hair the way Suzy brushes yours, and he could always make her happy, so I figured he couldn't be held to fault for his family all bein' driftwood and if your momma loved him, it was good enough for me.

"If they'd'a had a son, he'd'a been king, but the fish boat motor blew up and they only had time to strap a life preserver on you and they were gone. Right out there in the bay.

"If she'd'a been raised to run and swim insteada bein' in residential school, or if she'd'a trained for her puberty swim insteada learnin' bible verses, she'd'a easy swum home to me.

"But she didn't." Granny stared at me so hard I got goose bumps all over, and shivered. "So you're all I got left in the whole world. I'm Queen Mother of nothin' and Old Woman to nobody, and when I die, it'll all die with me.

"Unless," and she grinned suddenly and pulled Liniculla onto her knee, "unless this one's ears are as big as her eyes."

WOLF MOTHER

The male wolf Saqual was terrified, but he had seen the strange
woman creature come from the pelt of his beloved, and so he did
not flee...

Two large grey wolves ran from the forest, stopped at the riverbank and lowered their heads to drink water. First one would raise its head to check for danger, then the other, and both of them moved their ears constantly, listening for any sound that might mean something was sneaking up on them.

Their thirst slaked, the male lay on the rocky bank, enjoying the early spring sun on his body. Both wolves still wore the heavy coat of winter, and though it had been a hard, cold time, with lakes trapped under ice and only the fast-moving streams flowing freely, they were well fleshed and healthy.

The female stepped into the water and her slanted yellow eyes fixed on the far bank, her nose sniffing, sniffing eagerly. She yipped, and moved deeper into the water. The male whined, but the female made no move back toward the rocky bank. She stepped deeper, ever deeper into the river, until she could no longer walk but was swimming.

The male stood, raised his head and howled, but his mate

didn't answer. Frantic, he went into the water after her, and swam behind her as she crossed the river, which they had never before crossed.

The female was the first to step from the water and walk out onto the glittering black rocks. She shook herself several times, water spraying from her thick pelt, then she turned to watch as her mate, exhausted and trembling, came from the water and fell on the rocks, unable to walk, panting heavily. She moved to him, licked his face, made soft sounds to him and lay beside him, cleaning him, licking him dry. After some time he managed to get to his feet and stumble after her. She slowed her pace so he could keep up, and together they moved along the bank.

Twice they stopped so the male could rest, and then the rocks along the river changed from black to grey, and then from grey to soft brown. Sticks and bits of log were trapped in the crevices between rocks, showing how high the river got in flood time, and more than once the female pushed her nose into holes in the sandstone, where the river had carved some caves. But none of them was what she was looking for, and she continued up the river's edge.

Just as the sun was starting its long, slow slide down the western mountains, the female moved into a cave and did not come back out again. The male whined, and waited, whined some more, then went looking for her.

The cave was large and roomy, but there was no sign of the female wolf. The male sniffed the floor and followed her scent to the darkest back corner of the crescent-shaped lair. There, where only the sharpest eye would ever see, was an opening, a tunnel leading back into the blackness. The male wolf yipped, and from somewhere beyond the tunnel he heard the female answer.

Emboldened, he moved into the slit, his nose trembling as he tested the air. He moved carefully and steadily along the hallway to where the earth again opened into a vast cavern, where the female wolf lay on her side. The male moved to her and nudged her with his muzzle, and she licked his nose in greeting. Her body clenched, her back legs drew forward, and a slight grunt of exertion came from her mouth. The male settled beside her, worried and attentive, and each time the strange spasm afflicted the female, he washed her face, made soft sounds of encouragement and reassured her with the warmth of his presence.

The first wolf cub to emerge from its mother's body was grey, like the parents. The second cub was sandy coloured, like the cave in which she was born. The third wolf was black, black as the darkness into which she was born, and the fourth cub was white from one end to the other, except for her black nose. Other cubs arrived, in other colours and combinations, until there were twelve of them whining and nuzzling at their mother.

In the large cavern was a small pool of melted icewater, and the female left her litter with the male and moved to drink deeply of the fresh water. She shook herself several times, then drank again, and, her belly full of water, went back to curl around her babies. The water she had consumed became milk and the small, still-wet, blind cub puppies nursed from her until their bellies were full, then they slept between the warm bodies of their parents.

The female and her brood were still asleep when the male left the big cavern and moved down through the tunnel and through the smaller guardian cave. Squinting against the light, he moved carefully to the mouth, peered out and checked the wind before leaving the safety of the shelter. He disappeared into the thick dark forest and began hunting for food for himself and for the family still sleeping in the cavern.

A wolf has no pockets and no hands, so it can carry food in only two ways. When the male returned to the cavern he had a large, heavy haunch of deer gripped in his teeth, and he had a bellyful of fresh, delicious deer meat, which he cast up for his family. The female ate and ate and ate until her belly was stuffed, and only when the male knew for certain that she was satisfied did he finish the last bit of his offering himself. Then, together, they chewed and gnawed the haunch, even cracking open the bones and licking the rich marrow. They did not feel hunger, but nature has determined they must feast when food is there and store fat for when there is no food. They slept, and the puppies slept, then wakened and drank rich milk, then slept again. When the parents wakened, they finished the haunch, then licked each other's faces clean and rested some more.

After a while the female wolf rose from her litter and moved down the cavern to the tunnel, through it to the cave and, as the male had done, stopped at the opening to test for danger before leaving the cave. She ran along the riverbank, stretching her body, loosening her muscles. She went into the forest, sniffing, examining, exploring her new territory, and when she was far enough from her whelping lair to know it was safe, she dug a hole and emptied her bowels and bladder, then covered the hole again. She ran back to the river, went in it and swam until the water had cleaned all scent of birth fluids from her hide. When she was completely clean, she ran as fast as she could back down the riverbank to the guardian cave in the sandstone.

The pups were all awake and whimpering, trying to get from their father that which can only be obtained from a mother. The female wolf lay down with them and curled around them, and they pushed close to her, searching for and finding her nipples, sucking hungrily. Those who couldn't find a teat whined unhappily, and had to wait until the others were satisfied, then push in for their feed.

The male waited until the pups had quieted and begun to sleep, then he rose and slipped out, a shadow in the darkness. He was gone a long time, and when he returned his belly was again distended and in his mouth he gripped two fat rabbits. He made his offering to the female and she ate eagerly, then they lay together with the pups warm between them, and rested.

When the pups were two months old, the parents led them from the darkness of the cavern to the guardian cave. The light frightened the little ones, and they cowered in the darkest corner, but their mother pushed them to the middle of the cave and their father kept them there until they were used to the light pouring in the mouth of the smaller cave. Their ears twitched when they heard birdsong from outside, their little noses wiggled as they tried to sort out the many scents coming to them. The male stayed with them while the female went out and into the woods to dig a hole, do what her body demanded, then fill the hole. And when she had done that, she went hunting.

She ate until her belly was almost dragging on the ground, then dragged as much of the deer carcass as she could manage to the small cave. The pups nosed at the fresh meat, even tried to gnaw, but their teeth were still like needles and they had little strength in their jaws. When they were ready to give up their vain attempt to consume fresh meat, their mother cast up a pile of mostly digested meat and the pups lapped it up eagerly. With the food they got digestive enzymes from their mother's body, with which they could use the nourishment. They were still feeding when the male wolf left the cave to backtrack the female, find what she had been unable to carry, and bring it back.

Within a week the pups could rip small bits of fresh meat from the kills their parents brought to the cave, and by the end of their third month they were eating whatever came their way and no longer needed to nurse from their mother.

One summer day the wolf family left the cave and followed the river downstream to where it emptied into the ocean. The pups raced back and forth on the sand and ran into the salty water and back out again, pretending a fear they did not feel. They found and crunched down small crabs, shell and all, they snapped at and even caught small fish left behind in pools when the tide had gone out, they chased after gulls, they dug down after clams then raged when they couldn't open the shells. This one or that one would flop to the dry sand and sleep, but only for as long as the others allowed. Sooner or later another cub would go to the sleeper and begin to tug at a foot or gnaw on a tail and then the sleeper would come awake and pretend to fight.

The female went into the ocean and swam, then came from the water dripping and clean. She shook herself, shook some more, then shed her pelt and lay it over a bush to dry. Woman walked back into the ocean, swam in a new way, came from the ocean and moved to lie on the sand with her head resting on the powerful body of Saqual, the male wolf. He was puzzled, he was terrified, but he had seen this strange woman creature come from the pelt of his beloved and when he sniffed her, she smelled as she should, and he did not flee. Besides, his puppies were playing nearby, and he would die rather than abandon them.

After a while some of the puppies moved to Saqual and lay beside him, staring in wonder at this new creature. One of the puppies carried over a clamshell, and the woman took it from him and rapped the hinge on a rock, breaking the muscles that hold the clam shut. She pried off the shell and offered the cub the nugget of flesh living inside. The pup licked it from her fingers and his mouth was flooded with the wonder of clam taste. When he lifted his head to howl his pleasure, his pelt fell off and a little boy was sitting beside a wolf and a woman. "Ma," he said, and moved to the woman. She held him in her arms, stroked his arms and legs, made him comfortable in his new skin. Then, together, taking with them the little boy's former skin, they moved down the beach accompanied by two more cubs.

The cubs dug where the woman indicated, and each time they dug they exposed clams. The woman gathered them and stored them in the discarded pelt of her son. When the pelt could hold no more, they walked back to where the puzzled Saqual was lying with the rest of the cubs.

Again and again the woman cracked open clams, again and again she offered the clam meat to the cubs and again and again the cubs licked the meat from her fingers. Three more cubs shed their pelts and became human children, but the others remained as they had been born.

When the light began to fade, Saqual rose, shook sand from his pelt, and began to walk back up the river toward the cave. The wolf cubs followed him. The woman and her four children stayed on the beach. They ate more clams, they drank fresh water from the river, and they slept that first night under a thimbleberry bush—a grown woman, two little girls and two little boys, their lips stained with berry juice, their bellies full of clam. And, in the same way the cubs had been born with different colours of fur, the four children had different-coloured skin; one child was brown, one was sandy yellow, one was white and one was black. They were brothers and sisters, born of the same mother and father, but not identical.

In the morning, Saqual and the wolf cubs came to the beach to visit with their relations. They found Woman and her children sitting beside the river, feasting on fish. Woman offered some to Saqual and he ate from her fingers, enjoying his first taste of salmon. Woman lay on her belly, leaned over the river and sang a song of praise. Several salmon surfaced, lying on their sides, quivering with joy. Woman tickled them on the throat, then slid her fingers into their gills and lifted them from the water. Still singing, she offered them as food to

Saqual and the cubs, and they all feasted. Woman sang to the salmon and they offered themselves willingly, and when Woman and her children and Saqual and his cubs were no longer hungry, Woman sang for the salmon until they were so filled with joy they charged upriver to spawn in the gravel banks.

That first full day as human people, Woman and her children chose a spot above the river where it joins the sea. The water had already made a series of small caves but with Saqual and the pups digging, digging, digging, digging, one of the caves was enlarged, then enlarged again until it was large, and airy, and safe. That night Woman and her children slept in the new cave, while Saqual and his cubs went back to the first cavern and curled together in the comforting darkness.

Some days Saqual and the cubs brought deer meat or rabbit, grouse or pheasant, and other days Woman charmed the salmon, but every day they all, wolf and human, ate their fill.

When summer was finished and the storms of autumn began to howl, Woman and her children wrapped themselves in the pelts they had shed. They learned something new every day; how to make fire, how to weave nets, how to make fishing line, how to fashion a hook, how to cook cod and perch and trout and even the bigmouth sturgeon.

One day, when he was out hunting, Saqual encountered a female wolf. She was rake-thin and limping, and looked as if she would soon die. He questioned her and she told him she had been attacked by a cougar and so badly wounded she could no longer hunt. Saqual took her back to the cavern with him and fed her, and while she lay sleeping with his cubs guarding her, Saqual raced down the riverbank to the beach, where Woman was gathering oysters.

Saqual went to Woman and licked her hand. Woman stroked his pelt, petted him, scratched behind his ears and under his chin. Saqual told her of the female wolf, and how he had taken her back to the cavern. Woman smiled at him, and again stroked him, until he was so overcome with joy at the sensations her hands caused him, he lay on the beach and whined happily. The boys and girls who had been his cubs came to him, and tumbled with him, playing and laughing and doing as their mother did, stroking his lovely pelt.

When Saqual went back to the cavern he went back as a lone wolf, not the mate of the she-wolf who had become Woman. And when the second she-wolf was healed, and well, and able to hunt again, she chose Saqual to be her mate, and by springtime there was a new litter of wolf cubs in the cavern.

Saqual took two of the pups to the beach with him, a male pup and a female pup, and Woman cracked open clams for them, offered the flesh to them, and they licked her fingers clean. Their pelts fell off and they were children, a boy and a girl, smaller and younger than her own children, with slightly different features, related to but not full siblings of her own. Still, she cuddled them, she stroked them, she made them feel at ease in their new skins, and when they learned to speak they called her mother.

WARRIOR WOMEN

"We knew we couldn't stay out in the open without bein' wiped out. It was a time, a time of change, a time to wait and do nothin' until we could see what needed done. So the women's warrior society went secret, as secret as the society of women..."

There are days on this island, especially in autumn and wintertime, when the clouds sit blocking the sun and the rain falls until you feel as if the sound of it hitting the roof is the only sound you've ever known, a sound driving you into yourself, hammering at your head until you think your knees are going to buckle. Just when you're sure you can't stand another minute of water, cloud, mist and fog, the wind shifts, the sky clears, and you'd almost think it was springtime.

We'd had nearly three weeks of rain and mud and were making jokes about watching for an old man in a long robe, going around collecting pairs of animals. Frankie Adams insisted he'd seen the old fellow, in gumboots, with an umbrella, trying to talk my dog Lady into going in a big boat, but Lady wasn't having any of it, so the old guy left. The kids had been in and out of the houses so many times the women were ready to lock the doors, and we all had flooritis from wiping up after muddy feet. Kids would come in from playing in the puddles soaking wet and smeared with mud, and they'd no sooner get into dry clothes and warm up a bit than they'd be outside again, leaving the laundry problem a bit bigger. We had clothes drying on lines and hooks, steaming up the windows and making us all feel even more hemmed in, and then the sun broke through and the rainbows started forming in the sky and we all went out to look at them.

"Just like the wings of dragonflies and butterflies," my Granny smiled, nodding her approval. She was sitting on the porch, feasting on the glory even with her fading eyesight. We moved the washtubs into place and started the fussy old agitator machine on the porch, and got busy with the jeans and socks and heavy sweaters we hadn't been able to get clean washing by hand, and Liniculla helped me fill the rinse tub with cold water. We were barely into the first load when Granny started to talk, the soft flow of her voice counter-pointed by the chug of the washing machine, the swish of the hot wash water against the stiff denim.

"The Fireweed Clan were the nurses," she told us. "Most of their women were disciples and the old woman would figure out what needed to be done for a sick person and mostly it was the Fireweed Clan would do the tendin' and carin'. When the epidemics hit, the Fireweed Clan was the worst affected and even though they knew it was almost sure death, they still looked after the sick. It was what they'd been trained to do, it was what they had always done, and even if the world was endin', that was no reason to stop their purpose in life. So many of them had died, there didn't seem to be enough left to continue as a clan, so they sang the songs, said the prayers and retired it, and were accepted into other clans. Some are Bear Clan now, some are Eagle Clan, some are Killer Whale, some are Wolf, but we still know who was Fireweed because their families still got the right to wear the butterfly design, or the dragonfly, or the bee, or the hummingbird."

She flashed a special smile at Liniculla, who was helping me by lifting jeans from the rinse water and feeding them through the wringer. And Liniculla grinned happily because now they both knew that when Granny got finished embroidering the butterfly-in-four-colours onto the dance vest and gave it to Liniculla along with one of Granny's own special names, there would be something extra being told to all the people. The people would see Liniculla dancing in her vest, and hear Granny give her the name in a ceremony, and they would all know that even though she came from Suzy's body and not mine, even though Suzy was no blood kin to us and her blood and mine would never and could never mix to start a new life, we're both parents in Granny's eyes, and Liniculla was entitled to be considered Granny's great-granddaughter, inheriting from her as well as from Suzy's grandmother.

Liniculla has never known any of the women of the family of the man who planted the seed in Suzy's body. But she won't grow up without a full set of relatives because now she has all of Suzy's and all of mine, and she will know who she is and where she came from, so she'll know where she's supposed to be going. She knows she is of the retired Fireweed Clan, with a loving history of service and healing, and that the rainbows were in the sky to remind her that nothing is ever destroyed completely, and the spirits of those who sacrificed themselves live on, coming together with the rain and sun to be a promise for us all. And when she dances in the vest with the butterfly-in-four-colours, all the people will know, too.

Granny had her hippie gear on, and we teased her about it, called her the oldest surviving flower child on the island and asked, did she want a plastic flower to tuck into her headband, and she just laughed at us and waved her fingers for us to keep feeding jeans through the wringer. She didn't always wear her hippie headband, just sometimes the mood would strike her and she'd put it on, tying her hair back with the black cord at the back. It looked like once it had been a hanky or a piece of cotton left over from a shirt or a dress, plain red cotton folded and knotted at the back. And through the knot, with both ends hanging down, and decorated with some old trade beads, was this black ribbon or cord she used to tie her hair out of the way.

We'd finished the wash and emptied the machine and had all the jeans and heavy socks hanging on the line, flapping in the stiff breeze from the sea, and some of the older women came over to have tea with Granny. You could tell they'd been washing, too, their hands were still puffy and wrinkled from the water and they had their hair held in place by hippie headbands, too. There was a blue one with white dots you knew had been a handkerchief, a sunshine yellow one, and my stand-in granny, in case my own died and I needed help or counsel, was wearing one that was orangey-red with a white flower pattern.

Granny went into the house with the old women, Liniculla went off to join her friends sailing little boats in the puddles, and when Suzy and I finished hanging up the last of the washing, we went inside. The old women were sitting around the kitchen sipping tea, talking their mother language and laughing softly. Suzy and I got cups and tea and sat listening, not participating, and I enjoyed, as always, how my Granny was around these old women. She seemed freer, more relaxed, she chose her words less carefully and laughed more often, as if she felt safer with them even than with us.

"Not all fishers are skippers," Granny said suddenly, "but all skippers are fishers. In the time before the strangers came, women were fighters same as men, and got the same trainin'. Not all members of the women's warrior society were members of the secret society of women, but all the members of the secret society of women were members of the warrior society. A woman warrior recognized the face of the enemy and was prepared to do whatever was necessary to defeat it.

"Sometimes the women warriors met without the men, to sit in a circle and talk woman talk, and if a woman had somethin' botherin' her, or puzzlin' her, or scarin' her, or makin' her feel uneasy, she'd say what it was. She could take all the time she needed to talk about it, but it was expected she'd have put some of her own time into findin' the words and not talk in circles, endlessly, takin' up everyone else's time.

"Then the other women in the circle who had maybe had somethin' the same happen in their lives would talk about it, and about what they'd done, or hadn't done, or should have done, and sometimes out of it would come an answer for the sister with problems. And even if not, sometimes it was enough to just have been heard and given love.

"It was expected that besides just talkin' about what was

botherin' you, you'd *do* somethin' about it. Usually it's better to *do* almost anythin' than let things continue if they're botherin' you. But sometimes the best thing you can do is nothin'. Sometimes you have to wait for the right time before you can do.

"A woman would come to the circle as often as she needed, but the circle wasn't there to encourage a woman to only talk about her problems. The first three times you came with the same story, the women would listen and try to help. But if you showed up a fourth time, and it was the same old tired thing, the others in the circle would just get up and move and re-form the circle somewhere else. They didn't say the problem wasn't important, they just said, by movin', that it was *your* problem and it was time you did somethin' about it, you'd taken up all the time in other people's lives as was goin' to be given to you, and it was time to stop talkin' and *do* somethin'.

"A woman might not know what was botherin' her. And it was fine to go to the circle, or even to ask to have one formed, and just sit with women, and listen and maybe get strength from smiles and cuddles and just bein' with women you knew loved you.

"A warrior woman had to be able to recognize the face of the enemy or she couldn't be a warrior woman. Anyone who just dithered around like a muddlehead and didn't *do* anythin' about her problems would have her warrior headband taken away and she'd have to start all over again, tryin' to qualify to get it back. Nobody with a drinkin' problem could be a warrior. There wasn't any drinkin' problem before the others came, but after they were here, some people had their headbands removed when we all saw they couldn't stay sober. A person who couldn't control her bad moods or temper would lose her headband until she learned control, because ragin' around at nothin' is wastin' energy needed against the enemy.

"When the foreigners came and the sickness started, the warriors got hit bad. The healers and Fireweed Clan women had been in the secret society and were the backbone of the women's warrior society, and they were gettin' the worst of it all. Soon there were hardly any women left in the warrior society, they'd died fightin' the Keestadores, or the sickness or age took them and there weren't many young women to take over from them. Since there were less and less young women in the warrior society, women from other clans were recruited into the secret society.

"We knew we couldn't stay out in the open without bein' wiped out. It was a time, a time of change, a time to wait and do nothin' until we could see what needed done. So the women's warrior society went secret, as secret as the society of women. Only the women in the warrior society knew who the others were. It was the only way to keep the secret safe.

"And for four generations it's been a secret. Only the most trusted of the sisterhood knew that some of us wore a band for more than to just hold our hair off our faces, or be a decoration. And sometimes women without the right would wear what we called princess headbands, but the warrior women always knew who was and who wasn't entitled to wear the mark. And it helped keep the secret. If people thought it was just fashion, like lipstick or brassieres or pointy-toed shoes, there was less chance of the truth bein' found out.

"And now it's a time of change again. Time to change.

Women are recognizin' the enemy. Women are lookin' for truth. Speakin' to young women, tellin' them that rape isn't anythin' at all to do with love or even with lust, tellin' them it's just another way for some people to convince themselves they've got power, any old kind of power. Women are learnin' to use their bodies again, learnin' to defend themselves again, and speakin' the truth about alcohol and pills and body shame. Lookin' for truth, lookin' for support, and love, and a circle to join."

Granny took off her headband and held it in her old hands, smiling at it as if it was a living friend. "The black ribbon is the Death Cord," she said proudly, "the sign of rememberin', rememberin' all the women who have died to protect the soft power. White women burned as witches, black women sold as slaves, yellow women crippled and sold like furniture, brown women raped, their bodies made sick with disease, murdered. The beads are special, each has its own magic, its own power, four on each end of the Death Cord because four is a full number, a true number. The Death Cord could be a shoelace and it would still be what it is, a mark of rememberin' all the sisters who came before us," and she put the old red cotton band back around her wrinkled brow, pulled it down and fastened the Death Cord around her bun again.

I looked at Suzy and thought of her own fight for life, the years of confusion, pain, the drunken parties, the time spent with foster parents, the years away from the village, going to the city schools. She got herself so buggered up in her head that Granny went to another society and got Suzy grabbed, and then came months of testing in the Big House.

Getting grabbed is scary, and it's probably the hardest thing a person will have to do in her whole life. Without warning, you're surrounded by figures with masks, so you don't know who anybody is. When you've grown up knowing the faces of all the people in the village, it's terrifying to all of a sudden not recognize anybody at all. And the dancers take you to the limits of what you can stand, they bring you face to face with every fear you ever had, and just before you go crazy, they lead you back. With song and dance and ritual and magic, they lead you back from the very edge of total insanity so that nothing can ever really scare you again. You've seen the faces of your own worst fears, and lived through it, and come back, and from then on you know your strength.

My eyes were full and I could feel the tears on my face, and I knew the senior sisters could see, and share, what I was feeling. If ever anybody had to fight for survival, it was Suzy, and if ever anybody won a victory, it was her. It was after being grabbed that Suzy cleaned up her life, went to university, studied hard, and finally became a paramedic. Bringing her baby Liniculla, she came home to work for her people, going to the small ports, and villages, healing the sick and comforting the sad. She's been everything to me all my life, best friend, secret-sharer, chosen sister and crying shoulder, and even when she was lost, confused and frightened, her courage never failed.

We all had another cup of tea, and then the old women left, and we started supper, and then brought the washing in off the line and hung it up on cords in the house to finish drying. Suzy and Liniculla stayed for supper and we all went to bed with the jeans, socks and sweaters still hanging in the house, steaming up the windows and making the place smell like the outside breeze was trapped inside.

In the morning the rain was back, and I woke up feeling grumpy, listening to the sound of it on the roof. Suzy was still asleep, curled up like a kitten, and I could hear Granny and Liniculla in the kitchen, chattering together and starting breakfast. I didn't want to get up, but then Suzy opened her eyes and saw me glaring at the rain, and she put her foot against my back and pushed, so I was out of bed whether I wanted to be or not.

"Somethin' came." Granny motioned with her head, handing us each a cup of coffee. Just in front of the door were two brown paper bags, like the ones the kids take their lunch in to school. One of the bags had my name printed on it in pencil, the other had Suzy's name. It looked as if sometime during the night someone had opened the front door, reached in, put the bags on the floor and left again.

I opened the bag with my name on it and brought out a folded red cotton hanky, knotted at the back, with a black shoelace dangling from the knot. I held it, staring stupidly, unable to find words.

"We're recruitin' again," Granny said contentedly, laying bacon slices in the black cast-iron frying pan. "Invitin' women who recognize the face of the enemy and are willin' to do somethin' about it to join us. You don't have to," she added quietly, "if you don't feel ready to shoulder the load. That's your choice."

Suzy left the house and came back with the eagle feather her grandmother had given her before she died, and she sat sewing while the bacon and eggs cooked and her first cup of coffee grew cold. She replaced the shoelace with a length of black ribbon, and passed it through the knot of her blue headband. I beaded my shoelace with big blue trading beads. Then, feeling scared and proud and a lot of other things, I handed the headband to Granny, while Liniculla watched enviously.

"Granny?" was all I said, but she knew what I wanted.

She waited while I turned so my back was to her, and I scrunched down, because she's lots shorter than I am, and then Granny put my headband in place and fastened the Death Cord around my braid, and gave me a little pat on the head.

"That's it," she said, and I don't think I ever heard her sound more content.

Suzy looked as if she was feeling all the things I was feeling. She kind of gulped, then handed her headband to Granny. She sat down quickly, blinking fast, and Liniculla and I grinned at each other as Granny's wrinkled old hands fussed, making sure Suzy's warrior woman band was just so.

"Looks good," Granny approved.

"Feels good," Suzy and I said at the same time.

And then we were all laughing and hugging each other and feeling so good that even the endless rain couldn't take the shine off the day.

THE FACE OF OLD WOMAN

"There's a power other than the power we live with every day. It's the power that taught levitation. It's the power that lets us leave our bodies and fly like spiritbirds…"

———

The rain bashed against the windows, the deep black night pressed close against the side of the house, like a hungry bear wanting to be allowed in to warm itself by swallowing the lamplight. The kettle was steaming on the big black wood-burning stove and the clic-clic-clic sound of Granny's knitting needles snapped through the music coming from the radio. Suzy was making her regular monthly tour of all the outports and villages, and she'd taken Liniculla with her to show her just what it was when Mommy packed her things and went away for a week to do Community Health Care Work, and to show her some of the places she went to when the Mickey Mouse radio started squawking in the middle of the night and Suzy started running with her bags for the speedboat Big Bill already had gassed up and waiting.

I was sitting at the table with my red-covered 250-page spiral notebook, trying to write down the stories Granny had given me permission to put on paper for the first time, and I was chewing the plastic cap of my pen, staring holes in the wall, not getting much down on paper at all.

"You look like someone who's havin' trouble," Granny invited.

I could have let it pass by making a joke about trying to find English words for our ideas and concepts, and even though she would have known I was evading, Granny would have accepted that. She was only inviting confidence, not demanding it. But I had been waiting for an invitation for days, and was glad to get it aired.

"I'm having trouble," I admitted.

"Want to tell me?"

She kept right on knitting, but her old eyes locked with mine, and I knew she already had a good idea of what I was chewing at myself about, and had known for almost as long as I'd been chewing.

"It's the stories." I put the pen down and talked to the third eye, the one few people use any more, the one you can't see but that exists, just up above the nose. "All these years all this has been kept secret. Anybody got a whiff of it and asked, we'd just smile and say, 'Secret Society of Women? Must be a real big secret, I never heard of it.' Being taught since I was little not to tell certain stuff to people, to give the anthropologists and ethnologists and linguists and such only the stuff they wanted to hear, giving them nothing at all when they came poking around asking questions. And now, all of a sudden, it's okay to put it on paper. Maybe even write a book and let other people know."

"Other women," Granny corrected. "It was up to us to keep the secrets because the longrobes wanted to destroy the truth.

Well, we kept it. Like a little bonfire, feedin' our lives like bits of wood, one or two at a time, keepin' it goin'. But it's not just ours."

Usually it's me gets up and gets the cups and the sugar and makes the tea. Tonight it was Granny, and I just sat and watched her, bustling around the kitchen, the short, pudgy, wrinkle-faced old woman who'd spent her whole life feeding a bonfire and most of my life looking after me. Lots of people would think she's kind of homely. She's as wrinkled as a dried apple, and years of walking have made the veins in her legs swell, and arthritis is getting into her joints so she walks with a bit of a limp, rolling like a fisherman first back from fishing, not yet used to the ground after days on a rolling deck. You look at her and you know it's been a long, hard life full of pain and tears. And I don't think I've ever known anybody as beautiful.

She gave me my cup of tea and went back to her chair by the stove, and I stared at the steam coming from the cup and tried to find some answers, and of course there weren't any.

"When the four families went off after the flood," she went on, talking but not looking at me, "they took knowledge with them, and I don't know what happened or what went wrong. I don't even know what all places they went to. But somethin' happened, because the knowledge got buggered. There's maybe bits of it all over, scattered bits, but most of it's lost. Only here, where it started, did the women manage to save most of it. But we didn't save all of it. When the sickness came, too many of us died, and what we've got is incomplete."

She was slipping in and out of English and our own language now, sipping her tea, watching shadows in the room only she could see, calling on the power to help her.

"This isn't stuff just for us, just for the tribes, and it isn't just for us in the society. This is stuff for all women: black women, from the grandchildren of Copper Woman who became the parents of the black people. Yellow women, they got the same grandparents as us when you go back far enough. White women, too, they came from the same belly, the belly of Old Woman. What did we save it for if we don't share? Fewer of us in the society every year. The old ones die and the young ones got educated by the invader, and they don't know, and we can't trust 'em enough to teach 'em all. Sometimes a secret can die, and sometimes a secret can kill. But a book, maybe some women will read it and they'll Know."

"Granny," I could hear the shaking in my voice, "if this gets put in a book and we find someone to print it...you know what's going to happen?"

"Sure," she grinned, "every expert in every university is gonna have a shit fit! Gonna be pointin' to all the books written by all the men and gonna say it's all a packa lies. Gonna scream that the books the men wrote tell the truth and this one's just make-believe."

"Granny, look what happened when we tried to tell them at the university that we'd travelled by dugout to the Hawaiian islands before Cook got there."

"Yeah," she giggled, "they wanted to know what year it was, and when we couldn't tell 'em on their calendar they said we hadn't been there. So what? This stuff isn't for the ones who cuddle the books fulla lies as if they were livin' things." She pierced me with her argillite eyes. "This stuff is for the women." She paused and stared at the stove as if something important was in it, the oven maybe, and if she could just reach it, touch it or smell it, she'd know something. "You told me they talked a language nobody could understand anyway! You told me it made you sick to hear all the stuff they said that made you feel like they had no respect for women, or for our people, and there you were, both, and so you wouldn't go."

"It's true," I defended myself. "I was there a year, four full seasons, and none of it even began to fit me. They talked as if they didn't have any connection to the words, like they were talking in circles or something. I went to classes, I studied, I wrote the tests and got good marks, and the whole time I felt like I was wasting my life."

"Good." She looked at me and smiled. "Good. I'm glad you came home. I missed you. And I hope they *do* say it's all bullshit. The women who can't find no peace in what the men's universities teach will maybe find peace in this."

"I'm scared." There, I'd put it into words.

"I know you are. I just don't understand why. So I'm askin'."

"They'll go to the politicians first. The professional Indians. They'll go to them and ask them if this is true. And most of them don't know about any of this."

"Lots of 'em do know," Granny corrected me. "They just been brought up that it's the women's business, and it's secret, and they kept it secret." She grinned suddenly, and looked younger than Liniculla. "And you better stop sayin' that word *Indian*, or you're gonna be in trouble. I warned you. You keep sayin' that and the word police're gonna get you!"

I got up and refilled our cups. I brought out some of what

Granny calls coffee cake and cut some slices. She makes it pretty much the same as she makes frybread, only she puts eggs in it, and extra sugar, and maybe cinnamon or lemon, with a cream cheese mix on top, and she doesn't fry it, she bakes it in the oven.

"What if they *do* say it's bullshit?" I persisted.

"Well, and what if they do? Their grandmothers told 'em not to tell anyone. Good men do what their grandmothers tell 'em. Don't matter *what* they say, long as *we* know."

"Granny, everything we ever had has been stolen from us. What if...." I just couldn't finish.

"Can't steal what's been offered with love." She looked at me as if she was disappointed, as if all those years of trying to teach me had been wasted, as if I was still a few bricks short of a load. "There's gonna be women jump up and start tryin' to make a religion out of it and tryin' to sound like experts and tryin' to feel big and look clever. They'll get tired after a while and give up, but the truth'll still be there for the ones who keep lookin' for it. You worry too much, Ki-Ki."

"You said it yourself. Even our own young women. We can't trust them all because of how they've been educated."

"Can't trust 'em to keep it secret," she agreed, "but if it ain't secret no more, there's no reason not to trust 'em. They're women. Some of 'em will be jealous that they weren't told, and they'll holler that it's lies, but we got to learn to hate what they're doin' and still love them. It's not their fault. They been educated wrong, is all. We gotta trust somethin'." She looked at me with tears in her eyes. "I'm tired, Ki-Ki. Deep inside me, in a place I never been tired before, I'm tired. I'm the old woman and there aren't enough sisters in the society to give me back the strength I need when I feel tired like this. I gotta have faith in myself. I gotta have faith in Old Woman. I gotta have faith in you and the thing you want to do. There's gotta be a reason that you been scratchin' stuff on paper since before your puberty. There's gotta be a reason that your writin' happened at a time when women everywhere was standin' up and sayin' they want to know woman's truth, no more longrobe bullshit."

She remembered her cup of tea and took a sip. She ate her coffee cake and nodded satisfaction at how it had turned out; she had never baked a bad one, but each time she takes that first taste, she nods, as if she's almost surprised that the recipe worked. She traded for that recipe, with a woman from Queen's Cove. I don't know what Granny traded and I don't know what personal adaptations she's made to the recipe, but I do know that it's the best treat a person could ever taste. "Sometimes," she said, licking her lips, "you just gotta trust that your secret's been kept long enough."

It felt good to me. I was just about ready to make another attempt to get words on paper. Granny got up and moved over to the stove to put in more wood, and she stood for a while, holding the lid up with the lifter, watching the firelight flicker. The smell of alder smoke drifted across the room. Then she put the lid back and hung the lifter back in its place. And when she turned to face me again, she wasn't my Granny any more. Her face was hard-edged, her mouth looked like the top of a drawstring bag that's been pulled shut, all puckered and lined, and thousands and thousands of years old. I stared into the face of Old Woman and felt the chair under me start to melt away, the table disappear, until there was just Old Woman, talking with my Granny's voice, but Granny's voice altered, just Old Woman and me, alone in a place that wasn't the kitchen of the house I live in.

"There's more," the voice filled my head. "There's a power other than the power we live with every day. It's the power that taught levitation. It's the power that lets us leave our bodies and fly like spiritbirds, and it's the power that allows Old Woman to be fog, or mist, or ride the wind, or speak through the old woman.

"This power has been around for a long long time, in more worlds than this one, on more earths than this one. And just as the opposite of fire is water, the opposite of hot is cold, the opposite of hard is soft, the opposite of man is woman, there's an opposite to the power that is good. And it's a power that is evil. And not everyone knows the difference.

"Our island sisters died of sickness, alcohol, confusion, and fear, to defend the soft power. Other sisters in other places died of torture, by burning, by drowning, by the cross-hilt sword, in defence of the soft power. All over this earth, for as long as there's been people, women have died to protect the secrets. If the enemy knows which of us know the face of evil, they attack. 'Thou shalt not suffer a witch to live,' and women die because the cold, hard power doesn't want women to learn we weren't made to be used and controlled.

"Women are bringing the pieces of the truth together. Women are believing again that we have a right to be whole. Scattered pieces from the black sisters, from the yellow sisters, from the white sisters, from us and our sisters, are coming together, trying to form a whole, and it can't form without the pieces we have saved and cherished. Without the truth we have protected, women won't have the weapons of defence they need. If we hold our secret to ourselves any longer, we help the evil ones destroy the Womanspirit.

"We must...we *must*...reach out to our sisters, all of our sisters, and ask them to share their truth with us, offer to share our truth with them. And we can only trust that this gift, from woman to woman, be treated with love and respect, in a way opposite from the way the evil treated the other things this island had. Rivers are filthy that used to be clean. Mountains are naked that used to be covered with trees. The ocean is fighting for her life and there are no fish where there used to be millions, and this is the work of the cold evil. The last treasure we have, the secrets of the matriarchy, can be shared and honoured by women, and be proof there is another way, a better way, and some of us remember it.

"There is more than one road to the afterlife, there is more than one way to love, there is more than one way to find the other half of Self in another person, there is more than one way to fight the enemy."

And then I was back at the kitchen table, and Granny was sitting in her rocking chair, staring at the floor, looking so old and so tired that I knew, suddenly and sadly, that Time for her was coming full. I got up, moved to the stove and added wood to the almost extinguished coals. I went to Granny and I held her, and she knew I was there, even though she didn't move or speak, and I went away from her to allow her time to come back into her own body, the body so recently occupied by Old

Woman. When the kettle was boiling, I made fresh tea for my Granny, and she smiled, and I kissed her cheek, and then sat down at my book to write.

I didn't hear Granny get up, I didn't see her refill my cup of tea, I didn't hear her slow footsteps as she headed off to her bed. I picked up my pen, stared at it for a few minutes, then I felt my face go hard, my mouth pucker, my body go cold, and when I came back to this world, the stove was out, I was chilled and stiff, my tea was cold and my pages were covered with what might be a poem, or several poems, or a song or several songs, or maybe all of that. And I knew then, and know now, that what we have protected on this island is not complete, the knowledge is scattered, and if we offer all women what we know, the scattered pieces can start to re-form, and those who need to find courage, peace, truth and love will learn that these things are inside all of us, and can be supported by the truth of women.

I am the sea

I am the mountains

I am the light

I am eternal

This confusion is fog
There is light beyond
I sense it and feel its warmth

I move toward it
but not headlong
I fear to stumble,
to fall with pain.

There are women everywhere with fragments
When we learn to come together we are whole
When we learn to recognize the enemy
we will come to recognize what we need to know
to learn how to come together

I know the many smiling faces of my enemy
I know the pretence that is the weapon used.
I have been the enemy
and learned to know myself well.

The ones who talk only from the throat
see only with two eyes
hear only with ears
but pretend to do more
are the enemy

I walk amidst shards
and fear laceration
I must dare to bleed
I must dare to cut myself
To amputate
the festering pain.

I will learn to mix
medicine bags for those with faith
I will learn to chant the power chant

I will learn to mix
medicine bags for those with faith
I will learn to chant the power chant
and play the healing drum.
I will not fear moss voices
       water songs
       small furry things with sharp teeth
       or my own hesitancy.

I am falling
I am falling
       past star
       past time
       through space
       and my own fragments

oh sisters the pain

I am scattered
I am scattered
       gather fragments
       weave and mend
       scattered fragments
       weave and mend

In golden light
I recognize the enemy faces
fear of our bodies
fear of our visions
fear of our healing
fear of our love

fear of sisterkind
fear of brotherkind
fear of fear

    love is healing
    healing is love

There are Women everywhere with fragments
    gather fragments
    weave and mend
When we learn to come together we are whole
When we learn to recognize the enemy
we will know what we need to know
to learn how to come together
to learn how to weave and mend.

Old Woman is watching
Watching over you
    in the darkness of the storm
    she is watching
    watching over you

    weave and mend
    weave and mend
Old Woman is watching
    watching over you
with her bones become a loom
    she is weaving
    watching over us
    weave and mend
    golden circle